THE GREAT
MONEY
TRICK

ANOTHER WORLD IS POSSIBLE

Mary Jackson

authorHOUSE®

AuthorHouse™ UK
1663 Liberty Drive
Bloomington, IN 47403 USA
www.authorhouse.co.uk
Phone: 0800.197.4150

Published by AuthorHouse   01/28/2015

ISBN: 978-1-5049-3512-8 (sc)
ISBN: 978-1-5049-3576-0 (e)

I'd like to thank my husband John for his patience and understanding in allowing me the time and space to write this book and my three children for their encouragement.

John Leadbeater and Julia Lynskey for their enthusiasm and support.

Immeasurable gratitude to Mike Forster, Alistair Tice, Ken Douglas and the Socialist Party for my political education and Robert (Noonan) Tressell for writing The Ragged Trousered Philanthropists, a book which changed my life and ultimately led to this novel.

Last but not least Sheila Kostyszyn a remarkable woman who gave me the inspiration to commit this script to paper.

Chapter 1

"Mum, dad, they're making a film about the miner's strike" Ellen shouted as she burst into the room. "It's gonna be brilliant. I've met the director, David Something. The BBC's paying for it. It's to be shown next year around the 20th anniversary. You two might be able to get in it as well, they're going to need lots of extras."

"Slow down. Start at the beginning and keep it simple "John said, putting down the crossword he'd been doing and smiling at his excited daughter. *25 year old and still jumping up and down like a child he mused. I hope she never grows up.*

Ellen laughed and sat down to explain. She had been out with her friends in the village, deciding where to go and someone had mentioned a film that was going to be made locally. Auditions were on that night in the pub at the top of pit lane. They'd gone along for a laugh but it had turned out to be interesting.

Ellen couldn't remember much about the actual miner's strike, she'd only been about 5 but she'd been brought up hearing stories about the great battle that the miners had fought to keep their jobs, she'd grown up with the harsh reality of watching her village change as more and more jobs were lost in the area, the pit closing, shops shutting down. Half her mates had never had a 'proper' job. The pit had opened again under a private contractor but only employed about 200 men instead of the 2000 before the strike.

The director had been brilliant, he'd explained that the BBC was funding the film about the strike and that he wanted it to be as realistic as possible. There seemed to be a lot of ex-miners in the group and the director had got them talking about how it had been. They'd done some bits of play acting around different scenes suggested by the old miners, reflecting actual happenings from the strike and been filmed while they did it.

Grace, Ellen's mother asked about the people who were there, maybe she knew some of them from her time in the miners kitchen during the strike. Ellen was a bit vague about names, she's recognised some faces but urged her mum to join her next week for 'rehearsals' but Grace was reluctant. "I can't just turn up I'd look stupid" she said but Ellen assured her that all the people who had turned up were urged to get others to join them, "especially people who had been active in the strike like you and dad".

Grace and John talked about it that night, talked about the strike and the things they'd done, it brought it all back and hesitantly they decided to go along just for a look.

Grace was sure that the true story of the miners' strike would not be told by the film, she'd never forget the way the media had 'stitched up the miners' even changed the sequence of the 'battle of Orgreave' and made out the miners had been the aggressors instead of the police. She could remember John coming home that day. He looked grey, he said he'd never been as scared in his life.

"They are determined to smash the strike" he'd said as he walked through the door. His jeans were torn, he was filthy, a gash on his forehead still seeping a bit of blood. He didn't stop for breath. He was more upset than angry at first, although that soon changed in the following weeks.

They both decided to go along and Tony their eldest joined them. Tony was three years older than Ellen and he could remember more about the strike, the 'Soup Kitchen' where his mum worked most days during the strike, the demonstrations, coach rides to London.

He'd been at school during the day but often ended up at the kitchen watching his mum and her friends prepare the meal for the next day. He'd enjoyed the strike, it gave him more freedom, he'd been allowed to stay at different friend's houses when his mum was away raising funds for the strike. He remembered the massive Christmas party they'd had, at the end of the party Ellen had said "Will you go on strike every year dad, this is brilliant"

Grace only went along to have her say if it turned out to be another whitewash of the police action in 1984/5 but she was pleasantly surprised, it seemed almost all her mates from those days had turned up, many like herself just to 'have their say' but after listening to the director, who it seemed really did want to know the truth and make sure the film reflected it, they all decided to get involved and enjoyed the rehearsal. Quite a crowd of them ended up in the pub afterwards talking about the film and about the good times they'd had in the strike.

To hear the men talk it could have been yesterday instead of almost twenty years ago, Grace was surprised at how many young people had been there, and not just to take part in a film, which was exciting in itself, but a lot of the younger lads had wanted to 'play their dad' in the film. As Tony said later, "it's not just you two who still go on about the strike, most of those kids wouldn't have even been born in the strike but obviously knew enough about what had happened to take an active part in planning the different bits of by-play that the director, David, had said were essential to the film being realistic."

He was even interested in Grace's little story about the time John had got despondent in the strike, Christmas was coming and they had no money for presents for the kids. She'd gone to her parent's and her dad had told her he'd known they had no money so he'd made a dolls house for Ellen and had almost finished a little garage for Tony. She'd been pleased but not as happy as John.

When she told him about the toys he'd told her some of the lads had been thinking about going back, they were all worried about being out of work so long, he had been worried about the kids going without at Christmas. He was so relieved.

She remembered it like it was yesterday and so had everyone else.

The filming was good fun but even the director seemed shocked at the way people felt, feelings were still as raw as they had been during the strike. Hundreds of locals had come forward to act as extras—but he couldn't get enough men to be policemen. In the end he had to bus in agency workers to play the 'enemy'.

Filming the last confrontation had been almost scary, pushing at the police lines, running from a police charge, the police baiting the miners. The bitterness and anger were still as strong as ever.

The director had to stop the filming to give us all a lecture. "This is a film, these are not police they are actors, IT'S NOT REAL." He almost shouted, there had been real aggression in the battles, a couple of broken fingers, some serious bruising, but we got it right in the end, final day tomorrow, it's going to be strange 'I'll have to find something to fill my time now' she was thinking when the door flew open and Ellen burst into the room followed by a few friends.

"We've been talking about the film, what a miss it's gonna be. We've all got used to actually doing something at night instead of watching telly or having a drink" she stopped for breath.

"Emma, Tom, Mandy, you know Sam and Paul, Sue, and Jane" she quickly introduced her friends. "We've all learned loads about the miners' strike, we grew up hating Thatcher and the Tories but Labour's been in power for years and it doesn't seem to be much better now. What is the answer? I've told them you'd help. Will you?"

"What did you learn from the strike?" from Tom.

"We really are interested" said Sam "it seems impossible that it really happened. Some of the stories we've heard have been incredible. A woman told me today that the village was almost in a state of siege for a time in the strike. She told me about one old woman that had been dragged out of bed by the police who had been chasing a striker and thought he's gone in to her house, she was very old and ill, she hadn't been out of her bed for three years, it's a wonder it didn't kill her. What was it like to have mounted police chasing you through the village? Unbelievable!"

Grace was a bit overwhelmed by the crowd but it wasn't so unexpected, she'd been watching them throughout the filming and knew they had been affected by what they'd learnt. "I've been half expecting this," she said "Although I must admit I hadn't expected you to all burst in here one night. I've thought about it and the strike did completely change my life."

"When the police took over the village it was terrible, your gran wouldn't go out, not to the shops, not even to the bingo. It happened without warning.

I wasn't here at the time but heard all about it later of course: it was a hot day, there was only ever a small picket on, no chance of scabs going in here, women and kids were stood about talking to the lads, the lads had been wondering why there were so many police but apart from that nothing unusual.

Suddenly the police line tightened up then mounted police charged up the road as the police line attacked, women and kids ran, the police grabbed pickets truncheons raised and just started battering them, mounted police chased pickets as they scattered. . . . . . terrifying! It hardened attitudes in the village and in the following days the police tried desperately to identify the lads who'd escaped.

Young Alan, I remember, not even a miner, just there talking to the lads, selling his Militant papers, a couple of coppers grabbed him, truncheon'd him and dragged him along the floor. There's some pictures upstairs. The photos were sent to Scotland yard, he eventually got a reply acknowledging it appeared to show an unprovoked attack but unfortunately none of the officers could be identified because their numbers were not on their uniforms! They would have managed to identify Alan if he had been the aggressor."

Grace went to the kitchen and put the kettle on then started to tell them from the beginning, about how initially they'd expected the strike to last a couple of months but no-one had thought the strike would last a year.

For Grace, the first thing that really affected her was when local pickets stopped the office workers going in a few days in to the strike so their final wage wasn't paid, it caused a few arguments between some of the couples they were friendly with and meant that lack of money was an issue from the start.

Grace suddenly got serious "The strike really did change my life and it happened almost by accident. It was about 4 weeks in to the strike when Laura, whose daughter Gina's the same age as Ellen, was talking to me outside the school gates about this great book she'd just read. All she told me was that it was about a painter in the early 1900s who was married with a young son and he was dying of TB.

I expected a good weepy about an artist but instead it was about a group of house painters, Owen the main character was a socialist and he was trying to convince his workmates that there was a better way to run society than how it was being run.

The book is set in a coastal town down south. The main characters work on various painting jobs together. Throughout the book Owen tried to persuade his workmates that their lives could be better, he answered all their arguments as to why they thought things couldn't be changed—incredible really, they were working in the most disgraceful conditions, sweated and harassed throughout the day, throughout their whole life. Existing on starvation wages—but they defended the system.

The Ragged Trousered Philanthropists by Robert Tressell explains how capitalism works, how it is based on exploitation and finally how society could be run so that everyone took part in making the wealth and everyone also shared the products of that labour and enjoyed the benefits."

Grace stopped suddenly "Sorry I got a bit carried away. It's the film that's got me thinking about the strike. But the strike for me was based on the new understanding I had gained from the book.

What do you want to know exactly?"

"Well I didn't know what I wanted when I came tonight but now I want to know about a book that can change your life" from Paul.

"That'll do for me too" said Jane.

They arranged to come round a few days later and Grace reached for the Ragged Trousered Philanthropists from the bookcase and started flicking through it to prepare for the discussion.

There was so much she wanted to tell them, eventually she decided to explain how workers are robbed of the things they make by means of 'The Great Money Trick' and possibly 'how society is organised' as the starting point and just see how it developed.

Chapter 2

On Monday Grace was a bit nervous, John had decided to stay in, which made her even more edgy and they had decided to split the talking, Grace to do The Great Money Trick and John would explain how society was run. Ellen and Tony had told them not to worry, their friends were all excited about it and had even persuaded a few more to attend. They were expecting 8 or 9.

At 7.30 their living room was crowded, the original seven plus Barbara (Babs) and Alan were scattered around on the floor and with Grace, John, Tony and Ellen there wasn't much room.

Grace started,

> I want to show how workers are robbed of the things they make, it's called The Great Money Trick in the book and the best way I can explain it is by using an old pit village, before pits were nationalised, as an example.
>
> The pit owner owned the pit and all the land around it, built homes (hovels) for the miners and their families and a shop. The men, their children too as they grew, worked down the pit. He paid them all with money but they couldn't eat the money

so they used it to pay the rent and buy food from his shop—before each week was up all their wages had been given back to him, if they worked really hard—which they were forced to do, the coal would pile up and the men would be laid off. The boss would have all his money back plus all the money he'd made from selling the coal, he still owned the pit and he had a stockpile of coal. The villagers had nothing because they'd given all their earnings back to the pit owner.

Of course he didn't evict them for non-payment of rent he very kindly allowed them to build up arrears and he also let them have enough goods from the shop to stop them from actually starving until he was ready to take them back on in the pit.

When they returned to work they owed him money and had to pay something off the arrears of rent and at the shop each week before they started spending on essentials so they were in a worse position than before because their money didn't go as far and they lived on the verge of starvation for months.

That is what's happening on a national and international level, the capitalist class as a whole exploit the working class—that's capitalism, on a vast and much more complicated scale of course but basically everything is created by work and the workers are not paid enough to buy back the goods they create.

There was a stunned silence for a few minutes, Ellen and Tony had heard it all before but for most of their friends it was a totally new idea.

Emma "I got a bit lost in that, the first part was easy but I can't see how it can be transposed on to such a large scale nationally never mind internationally. Can you join the two up a bit better?"

"Shall I explain how society is organised" said John "it might be better then you can all ask questions but I think it will be easier taking the two things together" there was general agreement so he started.

How society is organised

Everyone living uses the resources to a greater or lesser degree—society is made up of different groups of people.

Those who do no work—tramps and beggars, royalty, bankers, owners of industry, all those enjoying inherited wealth.

Those who do harm—thieves, swindlers, burglars, bank managers, financial advisers, share managers, shareholders, vicars and priests.

Those who do useless work—this is the largest section of all, salesmen/women, canvassers, insurance agents, the majority of admin workers, bank workers. A vast army of people engaged in advertising.

Those engaged in necessary work—The producers of all the benefits of life—At any one time a quarter of these are unemployed, underemployed, sick or caring for the sick, the young and the old.

So at any one time the only people engaged in useful work producing the goods are at most a third of the population

"Just a minute" said Sam" I work in sales and I can tell you I work very hard, there is so much competition, we have targets to meet every month and we get a really hard time if we don't meet them"

"And I don't see how you can say the royals don't do any work, they bring in loads of tourists, you've put them in with tramps and beggars. It just doesn't make sense" from Sue

"Well the tramps and beggars belong in the group that do no work, I don't think you can argue with that and I am talking about useful work, the work that produces the benefits for mankind—produces the goods and services that benefit us all." Rejoined John "and I don't doubt that you work very hard Sam but you are not producing anything, you are simply persuading people to buy one product instead of another or from you instead of another salesman.

It will become clearer if you give me a chance to finish.

So if you accept that the only people who produce anything, and I will come back to you on the things you've raised, are in the small group at the end then you can see how there could be shortages of things we need."

John handed out some pieces of paper he'd had copied at the library.

The Oblong

Those who do no work	Those who do harm	Useless work	Useful Work
Rich, titled, tramps and beggars, royalty, aristocracy, all those enjoying inherited wealth.	Thieves, burglars, swindlers, bankers, financiers, owners of industry, members of parliament and churches	salesmen/women, canvassers, insurance agents, the majority of admin workers, bank workers. A vast army of people engaged in advertising. Call centre workers and the majority of shop workers,	This group include the unemployed, sick & carers as well as all those engaged in production of the necessities of life

"There is no shortage just now in Britain, but on a world scale we see gross poverty and deprivation, millions starving in the third world, babies dying for want of clean water and food—sorry, I wandered off the subject—but the goods that are produced are not even shared out equally, the first two groups between them consume two thirds of the things produced"

"You've obviously never seen Sam eat" from Sue laughing

"It's not just a matter of how much they eat and drink, it's the fact that their clothes, furniture, houses and food are generally better quality than those of the workers. The holidays they take are more expensive, everything they use takes longer to produce, the waiters serving them and their own servants are not able to take part in the work of production because they are engaged in useless work serving the bosses"

"What about the tramps, I knew they didn't belong in the first group" said Sue grinning.

"Well let's leave them where they are for now, I know they don't do as much harm as the others in the group because they do indeed use much less of the resources than anyone else in that group but that's where I think they belong. They don't do any useful work and live from what others produce by begging for food and clothes instead of working.

Where was I? Yes, the people who produce nothing (the first two groups) share two thirds of everything that is produced and the people who produce everything along with the people who work very hard but are engaged in work that doesn't benefit anyone except in this crazy system called capitalism only have one third of all goods and services available.

Even within the groups it's not an organised 'fair share for all', generally the people who do work in the third group, work that is only necessary to the system we are living in, not necessary to produce the things we need, get a bigger share of the goods and services that are left than the ones who are actually producing."

"I was only kidding about Sam being a pig" laughed Sue.

"I know" John continued "but Sam gets a decent wage, much higher than the minimum wage and he can boost this with commission. Generally the people who work in the third group are better paid, live in better houses and enjoy more leisure time than the people who work in the factories and shops, cleaning the streets, working on the land etc. These are mainly on the lowest wages, live in cheaper houses, have less money to spend on leisure, take very few holidays, in fact use much less of the resources than the other groups.

So now surely you can see what's wrong with the system. A small minority create all the wealth in society but only get to use a few of the goods and services that are made"

"Well it makes a bit more sense now" said Tom "But I can't accept advertising is useless work. They do a brilliant job. If I want a new television I can spend ages looking at brochures, I can pick just the one I want. Check out all the features then go on the internet and find the cheapest supplier."

Tony jumped in then. "But the products will have brochures to describe the features. The advertising is to persuade you to buy from Comet or Miller Brothers or any one of a multitude of shops that sell the same thing. They don't add anything to the product.

Millions of pounds are spent on advertising. When you want a telly you could just go to the shop and pick one—but it's more complicated than that. There's loads of shops all selling the same thing. All spending a fortune that adds to the cost but doesn't add to the product—all determined to get hold of your money. Then there's the internet, more people trying to sell the same things, it might seem good for buyers just now as competition is keeping the price down but it's tripling the amount of work that's going in to the product but not adding anything to it.

The people in advertising are usually much better paid than the ones who actually make the product. If these people put their energy in to production we could more than double the things produced so more goods with the same amount of work."

"But then we'd have too many goods" Babs piped up "and all the workers made redundant. How will that help?"

"She's right" said Tom "It's bad enough now. I've had three jobs and been made redundant once, it was terrible. I'd worked there from leaving school but the factory moved production to Asia, workers there get paid a pittance. They work ridiculously long hours to earn enough to live, we can't compete with that.

I did get another job but it was only for a few weeks in a warehouse in December getting orders ready for Christmas, all I've had since then has been bit of agency work, it's terrible, the agency takes £25 off for travel before we get paid, there's no sick pay either."

"Ok" said John, "It's true that we have so called 'overproduction' but have we really got too many goods, too much food? Millions in the world don't even have the basic necessities of life, clean water, enough food to keep them from starving—but even if we ignore the third world, do we all have what we want or simply what we can afford?. There's loads of things need doing. People are managing without what should be the basics in the 21st century, a decent house, quality furniture, a good standard of living and regular holidays.

Taking Britain as an example. How many of you would want a better standard of living if you could get it? Better facilities, somewhere to go beside the pub. According to official figures there's less people on the dole than for years, but as Tom's just been saying, it's really difficult finding work so what's happening? The government simply changed the way people claim.

Grace knows more about the benefit system than I do but basically the Tories changed the rules so 16 hours work was classed as full time therefore part-time workers can't claim Job Seeker's Allowance to make up a decent wage.

They brought in Tax Credits to make up the difference for parents, it drove down the numbers claiming job seekers allowance but didn't increase the amount of work that's done.

Tax Credits subsidise the bosses not the workers, it allows business to keep more of the profits and let's tax payers pay for it.

Employers would sooner have a more flexible work-force so agencies were set up. Agency workers don't have rights, they don't even get laid off at slack times, they're simply not required. Anyone needing some time off sick is simply replaced by someone else.

The shops are full of goods they can't sell—but most of us want things we can't afford, why? Because workers can't buy back the goods they create, because they're conned by 'The Great Money Trick.'

There was a stunned silence for a minute then Ellen laughed "I told you they were good didn't I?"

"Well you've given us a lot to think about" said Paul "I've never thought about it like that before, I need time to digest it." There was general agreement that they'd all enjoyed what they'd heard and Grace suggested they think about it and if they wanted to discuss it further then to let Ellen know and they could all come round another time.

Chapter 3

Sunday afternoon, Ellen was making sandwiches and Grace was putting out pastries and cakes she'd baked the day before. "Are they all coming?" she asked Ellen "I didn't think Sam was impressed when John took him up about his work in sales belonging in the 'useless' category and Tom seemed quite shocked when Tony argued against advertising being useful"

Ellen laughed, "There was a longer discussion about advertising and sales when we met up on Tuesday but Tony took them both on and, with reservations, they both decided it was a different view that they wanted to know more about. What have you got planned for today?"

"I'm not sure really, I rather think they'll have had their heads together and come up with questions and arguments against us. I remember what a hard time I had trying to get friends to even discuss it in the miners' strike. They all hated Thatcher and the police for trying to destroy the pits and the heavy handed tactics used against pickets but they weren't ready to accept the whole system was based on exploitation and greed. We'll see."

By 2pm the living room was full. John was out at his parents but was due back any time.

"Everyone got food?" Ellen shouted. "Ok mum, over to you."

"I'm pleased to see you all and I'm expecting most of you have plenty to say so, who wants to go first? Tom?"

"Thanks, I'm still not entirely convinced about advertising, how can we know what's available, what's the best, cheapest, most suitable? I've decided to think about it a bit more but I might come back to it later, Tony destroyed me last week so I'll leave it for now"

"Babs?"

"Well I've been thinking about it all week. I just want to know more. I'm not sure how we can change the system, it's mind-boggling but I've always thought there must be a better way to organise things. I know you only touched on the third world but it's a serious consideration, how can we justify millions of people, babies and children dying of starvation in the 21st century. It's obscene."

Paul jumped in next, "I just want to know more, I agree with Babs. There's no way babies should be dying of starvation or lack of clean water now-a-days. We can fly to the moon, the government are preaching 'healthy eating' because of the cost to the NHS of obesity in Britain, we've cracked the genetic code yet we can't feed the world. It's ridiculous!"

"Oh come on," said Tom, "It's because of their own governments that they're starving. They're killing one another, official's steal the money we give to help, they have so many kids there's no wonder they can't feed them all. It's not our fault that they're dying!"

"Anybody else?"

Jane, who didn't usually have much to say, came in quietly with "Well I was a bit shocked when John put the priests in the group that do harm. I can understand that they don't contribute to creating the things we need but I can't see how they do harm. I get a lot of comfort from talking to Father John, he's really nice and he's sympathetic if there's anything wrong."

"Well is that all? I thought somebody would have mentioned Russia or China" Grace said laughing.

"Well actually" said Jane, "That's exactly what my dad said when I told him about the discussion we'd had last week but I don't know enough about either so I wasn't going to mention it. I told him he'd have to ask you that himself, in fact I asked him to come with me but he thought it would be a bit pushy"

"He'd have been welcome but it's a bit crowded in here, if anyone else wants to come we'll have to find somewhere else to meet.

Anyway if there's nothing else I'll try to cover the points you've raised although Russia and China are a bit big for me I'll have a go but if you want more than I can give you you'll have to ask John, he's much more knowledgeable than I am on that. I was so afraid that it would come up that I mentioned it in relief really. I should have kept my mouth shut.

I'll take Tom's point first, advertising. John covered it briefly last week, it's a massive, lucrative multi-billion pound industry. It creates nothing. It does employ thousands of people including many low paid, but many more are paid absolutely ridiculous sums of money to persuade us to buy a particular product, from a particular supplier, use a particular firm. The person who actually made the product or will perform the service is generally low waged and works a lot harder than the well paid performers who take part in the advert. I'm not saying their performance isn't good, some adverts are excellent, but not every day for months or years.

The talent, actors, directors, scene painters, camera crew, all the energy that's put in to adverts could be more productively used to create something valuable, a good film, a musical or theatre show"

"Hang on" Sam interrupted "that's not productive work anyway, they may as well be making adverts."

"Well I see what you mean but I've probably given a wrong impression in our original discussion, there is more to life than simply creating enough goods to satisfy the basic needs of mankind. Initially creating enough to make sure everyone worldwide has sufficient to eat and satisfy their basic needs, a place to live, warmth, clothing etc. has to be a priority but once we've all got what we need then we will all want more than that, we need leisure, enjoyment, pleasure.

If we were all involved in production it would take a relatively short time to build enough houses create enough goods to fulfil our needs, even worldwide. Remember we discussed last week that, in general, in any capitalist, industrial country, less than a third of people are engaged in productive work and even though a third of the world is starving we actually produce enough food now to feed the world one and a quarter times. Mountains of food are destroyed just in Europe to keep the price artificially high.

Once the basic needs are met then we can all enjoy the 'fruits of our labour'. Initially I would imagine that we would all be required to do a full week's work, maybe a 35 hour week but we would still have enough time to enjoy the things we want to do such as watch TV, go to the cinema, out for a meal, visit theatres, museums, whatever we want.

Although I can see the argument I consider basic needs to be more than simply a roof over our heads, food and clothes, although in this crazy system these are seen as unattainable luxuries for about a third of the world."

"But surely if performing and theatre are now 'productive work' then churches and religion must be just as important" said Sue quietly to Ellen.

"Maybe you're right" Grace said picking up on Sue's point "but which church, which religion should be accommodated? There's so many. I know you are a Catholic so using that as an example, it's an exceedingly rich organisation, I'm not an expert but I understand the riches in the Vatican are worth more than the whole of the queen's wealth, and she's not short of a bob or two—hidden away to be enjoyed by a few privileged individuals. What good is it?

Mother Teresa has raised millions, possibly billions by visiting the 'poor starving of the world' and lobbying governments and rich individuals to contribute—none of the money she's raised has gone to feed the starving she pleads for, it's all gone either direct to the church or to build new and better churches to allow the poor starving to worship in. I'm not religious myself but I know enough about it to know that the Jesus in the bible did not go around raising money to build bigger and better churches to worship his 'Father' in, he fed the hungry and healed the sick. He gave the 'sermon on the mount' he didn't use any of the grand places of worship in existence at the time.

If individuals and groups want a place to meet and worship their God then there is nothing to stop them arranging that in their own leisure time, maybe making the case to take over the upkeep and running of existing churches but it's not part of the overall scheme of providing a decent life and standard of living for the whole of the population.

You are probably thinking that the same can be said of any of the leisure activities I've already mentioned and you are right of course, there is probably someone somewhere who would want any and every type of religion and every type of leisure, but none of what I am talking about would be possible under this present system that's run by a minority for the main benefit of that minority. I am talking about a system where the majority decide what is created for the good of the majority and where all have a say in how society is run through true democracy, through a voting system that is truly representative, from individual streets, to estates, to village and town, region then country. Where elected representatives would be truly accountable to the people they represent.

But I'm getting ahead of myself, sorry, back to the points you've raised.

The final point I think is the starving millions—a point close to my heart, I understand that a baby or small child dies for the want of clean water and minimum food every 5 seconds. Its 3.30, we've been here since 2 o-clock which means that over 1000 have died while we've been talking, I don't know exactly how many but I do know it's over 17,000 a day, about 121,000 babies and children under five die every week, over 6 million every year, it's horrendous. It's not good enough to say 'it's not our fault' 'it's not our responsibility' we live in a global capitalist world and capitalism is simply not working, it's not providing enough food and clean water to stop this unbelievable slaughter of millions of babies by denying them the minimum requirement to live.

The poorest parts of the world aren't industrialised so it's a much smaller figure that work to create or grow the necessary goods and food, millions are simply trying to exist without the resources to feed themselves and their families. They aren't involved in collective work because of the way society is run. The land and all it holds was stolen from them hundreds of years ago by means of the 'The Great Money Trick'.

Africa as an example is the richest continent in the world for natural resources but is probably one of the worst examples of starvation and poverty in the world. Not because the people are too lazy to work but because they are not allowed to use the rich abundance of the land.

We're often told that socialism or communism 'doesn't work', it's been tried in Russia and China and it failed.

Well although Russia started off well with the best intentions and organisation possible, it was plunged into a civil war, 21 countries of the world tried to stop the People's Republic but despite all the problems of the war industrialisation, full employment and an end to homelessness was achieved.

Neither Russia after Lenin's death nor China became societies organised and run by the majority of the population having a say in how things were organised so neither were truly socialist nor communist, but that aside both did have planned economies and full employment.

Originally soviets were set up in all areas, representatives from all walks of life made decisions on production and distribution but after Lenin's death these were closed down by Stalin. Many of the leading organisers were killed.

It's true that those two societies did not solve the basic problems of everyday life by everyone having a fair share of all they created because of the massive bureaucracy making all the decisions and the bureaucrats living in luxury while the majority lived much more basic lives but there was no-one starving on the streets like there is now in the former USSR under Capitalism.

I understand that after the fall of the Stalinist regime, with the restoration of Capitalism conditions became terrible, state pension and wages were paid months in arrears, old people were dying of starvation, a Russian steelworker who came to Britain a few years ago on a speaking tour with the Socialist Party told us how things were for him and his wife who was a doctor, both worked full time as state employees and their wages were so far in arrears that they relied on the food they grew in their garden to live.

I think it's a bit better now but state pensions are so low and so far in arrears that old people are living in abject poverty, they grow what food they can and stand on the streets trying to sell things they've made to supplement their meagre pension.

Both Russia and China had a planned economy instead of one run on 'market forces' there was full employment, no homelessness and state pensions on retirement. Food and production were planned to cater for the needs of the population and it worked better than capitalism is working there now despite neither country being run under workers control and management.

Even a 'deformed' worker's state, however badly run, was better than what capitalism has had to offer workers in the former USSR. China is now a mixed economy and I don't know how it's working but I know there are problems. Not a very satisfactory explanation but I did say before I started that I didn't know enough."

John came home at this point and Grace broke off saying she'd talked too long and suggested they have a break while she put the kettle on for a drink. John followed her into the kitchen and she caught him up on the discussion so far.

There was a general babble of conversation when they returned to the room, apparently Tom had picked up on the starving in the third world and the millions of pounds in aid Britain gave every year and Ellen had taken him up on it, explaining the nature of the aid given, a lot of it being given in out of date medicine and even baby milk, drugs that haven't and couldn't pass safety regulations in the West, even Thalidomide that had been used in Britain in the early '70s as anti-sickness medication for pregnant women which had caused terrible birth defects like missing limbs is now being given to people in Africa, not as an anti-sickness medication but it's practically impossible to ensure it is not be taken by pregnant women. All this dangerous stuff is being accounted for at its full original price and is a big part of the 'aid' budget.

John joined them in the sitting room, he'd been thinking about where the discussion would go and had gathered some up to date information.

"Well sorry I missed the first part of the discussion but I've got some facts and figures for you that should give you all something to think about. I've made some copies so don't worry about remembering it all.

We talked last week about how only a minority of people actually create all the wealth in society and how that wealth is stolen from them by means of The Great Money Trick. I know you struggled with the concept and how Grace's simple analogy could be transposed to life in the 21st century and the global markets that exist today. I'm not going to attempt to explain it all but I thought a few figures from two of the richest countries might help you to see that it is the only explanation of what has and is happening.

> **Britain is the fourth richest country in the world yet 14 million people live below the official poverty line.**
>
> **Over the last decade, under both Labour and Conservative governments, inequality has risen faster than anywhere else in the world apart from New Zealand, Britain is doing great but we have the biggest gap between rich and poor than at any time since records began.**
>
> **America, the richest country on earth! The wealthiest 1% has seen their income increase in real terms by 157% since 1979 and by contrast the bottoms 20% of Americans are earning $100 dollars less a year than in 1979.**

45 million live below the poverty line and over 40 % of Americans have no health insurance, no medical cover. Despite all the advanced technology available in the US more than 32 million people have a life expectancy of less than 60 years.

On a world scale 815 million people go hungry, more than half of the 12 million child deaths each year are caused by malnutrition and it's getting worse. According to the United Nations the poorest countries are worse off now than they were 30 years ago, on the basis of current trends, the numbers living in absolute poverty, that is on less than $1 a day, will increase by 10 million a year for the next 15 years.

I think Grace has already mentioned the 6 million babies, children under five, that die for want of clean water.

The aids epidemic has already killed 25 million people worldwide and is predicted to kill a further 68 million in the next decade not because it is untreatable but because the treatment costs money. In Africa millions of children have lost both parents, millions of orphans, what does the West do?

It has a conference of the G8, the richest 8 countries in the world, to discuss poverty, the conference cost enough to have made a difference if it had been spent on trying to rectify the problem instead of as a photo opportunity for the world leaders to pontificate and wring their hands and promise to make a difference by giving aid and even thinking about giving medication—in the next ten or twenty years.

It makes me so angry when I think of the farce!

In Britain in 2000 the highest paid directors of the top 100 companies earned 48 times more than their employees, at the end of 2001 four directors paid themselves bonuses worth £43 million. The fat cat bank executives have even ensured themselves great rewards for failure, a couple of years ago the top man at NatWest was given a £3 million golden handshake when he was sacked for incompetence and the chief executive of Sainsbury's got £1.2 million when he was fired.

In America the former boss of WorldCom, responsible for the biggest corporate fraud in history walked away with a pension pot of $1.5 million (£1 million) but 20% of the 17,000 employees at WorldCom, employees who lost their jobs as a result of the fraud have not received a cent of their wages.

All these figures came from a book called Socialism in the21st century by Hannah Sell, I've copied them out for you but if any of you want to borrow the book we've got a copy.

The Great Money Trick is alive and well it's just grown out of all proportion that it's almost unrecognisable."

There was a stunned silence until Tom burst out "My head's hurting, I need a break. But seriously John you've given me a lot to think about, I regret my comments earlier, Ellen had already shattered my complacency with the 'out of date and dangerous medicine and baby milk' but I had no idea there was so much poverty in Britain and America nor how bad things are in the poorest countries but the figures for the wealthy in society and how the rich are rewarded for failure is mind-blowing. There is no other explanation than a gigantic con. A Great Money Trick!"

There were murmurs of agreement on all sides but no-one had anything to add so they broke up after all agreeing they'd enjoyed it but no firm arrangement were made to meet again.

Chapter 4

Grace, Ellen and John were discussing the news, Tony had surprised them by announcing he was bringing someone home to meet them all, he'd asked Grace if she'd time to bake and checked John would be at home. It was the first time he'd done this, he'd had a few girlfriends but this seemed to be different. It was someone he'd met through a workmate, Ellen had met her a few times but didn't think she was from the village as she'd never seen her about. "She's a bit smaller than me, called Claire, lovely golden blond hair and a pretty face, she seems nice."

Claire came for tea on Friday and they all took to her straight away, she was quiet and friendly, came from a nearby town and her dad had been a miner until a couple of years ago when the Selby coalfield finally closed. He'd been made redundant and had re-trained as a lorry driver.

It didn't take long for the conversation to turn to the miner's strike. Claire had been interested in the film they'd all been involved in and she could remember the strike and had similar memories to Tony, the extra freedom, the days out on demonstrations, having baths at her grandmothers because they'd no coal to get hot water at home. She'd thoroughly enjoyed it and it had been years before she'd realised what a struggle it must have been for her parents to have survived for a year without wages.

Her dad was in the Labour party, he hated Tony Blair and was disgusted that the first two things he did when elected was the introduction of tuition fees for university and giving control of the interest rate to the bank of England. Claire had joined the labour party when she was eighteen but had not stayed long "Half the people who went to meetings seem to either want the local councillors to fix the street light outside their house, to get repairs done to their council house, their roads mended or some other trivial moans sorted out. The rest were either good committed socialists or careerists who were waiting for existing councillors to die or resign so they could jump into their shoes." She explained.

After tea, when he felt everyone had relaxed and seemed to like Claire, Tony announced he and Claire were getting engaged on her birthday in two months time. Everyone congratulated the couple and Grace and Ellen wanted to start planning the engagement party. Tony was pleased at the reaction, he hadn't really expected problems but he felt relieved that the announcement had gone down well.

When he took her home later she insisted on him coming in to formally tell her parents, Dave and Betty, too. They welcomed the news but weren't as surprised as Tony's family because they'd known about the budding romance for a while now. Betty suggested he invite his parents round to tea on the following Sunday and maybe they could all go out for a drink afterwards. Tony telephoned home, Grace and John were pleased so arrangements were made.

Grace and John had enjoyed the evening out, Dave and Betty had been good company and they found they had a lot in common. Dave, now a long distant lorry driver, explained how, with the announcement of the Selby coalfield closure, the government had put in a lot of money through the job-centre and Yorkshire Forward to help the workers of Selby coalfield so those who weren't old enough to retire were helped to make the most of any opportunities, most had retrained or enhanced their existing skills to find work outside the industry, some had even gone to Australia to continue mining.

The evening had gone well and they'd made a few plans for an engagement party, Claire had wanted it at the local club her parents used but agreed John could organise it so it would be near enough for both of Tony's grandmothers to go. Grace's mam hadn't been well lately.

Back home Grace started drawing up a list of friends she wanted to invite. Claire and Tony had been easy about who to invite, they had few shared friends and wanted both extended families to be there. She was getting a bit fretful, the first one to leave the nest. She didn't think Ellen would be far behind, her and Mark seem to be spending all their spare time together.

Chapter 5

Grace and her mother, together with Claire's mum and Nan were putting the finishing touches to the spread they had prepared for the engagement party while John and Dave were hanging a 'congratulations' banner for the young couple.

"It doesn't seem long since we were doing this for your wedding" gran said to Grace.

"It's nearly forty years" said Grace "but it does take me back. The spread's a bit more ambitious. What did we have? Ham sandwiches and butterfly buns? I was in such a tizz all day I can barely remember the food. I was just so relieved we'd got through the ceremony without anything going wrong. What a day!

People started coming in at that point so they all found seats. Most of their friends were there as well as Tony and Ellen's mates.

Babs came over to congratulate the couple and say hello to Grace and John

It was good to catch up with people and as usual a few came home with them afterwards. Tony had gone to stay at Claire's but Babs, Alan, Tom, Sam, Paul and Mandy were crowded into the sitting room.

"It's just like old times" said Babs to Grace, "I used to enjoy listening to you when you were trying to explain the system to us. I understand how the system works now but I can't see what I can do to change it or even how it can be changed.

I remember how surprised I was at the ideas you were explaining. I'd not been interested in politics nor economics at school, it all seemed too difficult but you were good, you missed your vocation, you should have been a teacher."

"Not really, I've only got one subject and my brand of politics would be seen as subversive to most school boards. I did enjoy those sessions though and missed them when you all drifted away. Not that I blame any of you. Labour had been in power for years and very little changed. The rich got richer and the poor got poorer, there isn't a political party worth the effort. None of them are offering anything different. Blair completely sanitised the Labour Party, turned it into a middle class party, there is so little to choose between them and the Tories. All that's left is the wishy-washy Lib Dems.

Things can't go on for much longer, though, the whole world is running on debt, it's due for a massive correction that will make people think. House prices are going through the roof, young people trying to buy are so stretched that they are living on credit.

Even the banks and building societies are overstretched. Repossessions are shooting up. The banks don't want the houses back they want your mortgage payments. I wouldn't be surprised to see banks going bankrupt in the coming recession. It certainly can't be ruled out.

I've just heard that Gordon Brown has invited Microsoft's Bill Gates, Jean Pierre Garnier of GlaxosmithKline and Lee Scott of Wal-Mart to join a panel of international business leaders to advise the treasury and a report on the future of the welfare system is to be written by an investment banker, David Fraud. There's no doubt that his 'expert' advice will be on how to drive the disadvantaged into low paid work.

What we need is a new worker's Party, a Party that will inspire a new generation, that will have policies to change things for the better for the majority instead of what we have now, a Labour government who have brought in a few extra crumbs in tax credits but who have governed over an increasingly unequal society. The gap between rich and poor is getting wider."

"But how will a new worker's party be any different? You are right that most people have no interest in politics. It doesn't seem to make any difference which one is in power. I looked at the origin of the Labour Party after I'd read 'The Ragged Trousered Philanthropists' and it started out with good intentions.

Clause 4 **'To secure for workers by hand or by brain the full fruits of their labour and the most equitable distribution thereof'** says it all. They started off well, created the NHS, increased pensions and improved social services but it's gone downhill rapidly since then.

I couldn't believe it when Blair wanted to get rid of it from the LP constitution. From what I've read about whenever Labour were in power they didn't manage to implement it very well. I would have thought if we had ever had a Labour government that brought about real change in worker's conditions they would have kept the support of the majority and the Tories would be finished but it hasn't happened."

John had been listening and couldn't help himself from interjecting "It's an absolute disgrace the way workers are being sold out. MP's wages are so high most of them have forgotten who they are there to represent. I used to feel sick when I was on the GMC, the general management committee of the local Labour Party.

The 'highlight' of the night was the MP's speech. He always started with 'Well I haven't much to report because I've been in foreign parts' then he'd laugh. I think the worst speech he made was just before Maggie started the privatisation programme. He advised us all to get shares in bottled water. Not a word about how he was battling against it in parliament . . . . because he wasn't. Just thought we'd be interested in how to capitalise on the government selling off our essential services.

I looked around to watch the greedy careerists taking note and the decent members showing the anger and outrage that I felt.

I've been thinking about how we stop the rot in a new workers Party. I do think the salary is important and an MP should have no more than the average wage of his or her constituency. That's what the Militant MPs in the 80's did.

Being subject to instant recall if enough people in the constituency are dissatisfied seems sensible too.

From my time in the Labour Party it was obvious that in the main the people who wanted to stand for the council were the careerists who were in it for what they could get and the shenanigans at selection time had to be seen to be believed.

The ruling caucus of existing and prospective candidates and officers used to pay subscriptions for a core of members. We only ever saw these when there was an important vote. There was an amazing array of oddballs plus the old and sick. They didn't exactly turn up in ambulances but I wouldn't have ruled it out if the vote was close.

It used to make me sick.

I remember when the leader of the council collapsed in a meeting, everyone was shocked, someone went to get cushions for the floor, someone phone an ambulance, the deputy leader slipped into an empty office to phone councillors who hadn't been in the meeting to canvass for support to be the next leader"

"Why didn't you stand for the council?" asked Tom

"Well they did ask Grace to stand for selection one year but she told them if she did and found evidence of the corruption she kept hearing rumours about she would expose it straight away. They didn't challenge what she said but it was never mentioned again."

They all laughed and shortly after called it a night.

Chapter 6

It was summer, 2008, Grace was still working for the local authority in the housing department, mainly in repairs although often moving across to help out in the homeless section—she hated that job, there were simply not enough council houses to house everyone, housing associations were useful but it took so much longer to get someone settled than in the 'old days' when she'd got married

Tony was married, they'd got a mortgage on a flat, Claire worked in one of the big stores so they could manage fine. Even save a bit. She had worked there since leaving school and they didn't want to start a family straight away so the mortgage was manageable. Tony was a painter & decorator and had been doing ok.

Grace was nearly 60, she was thinking about retirement, she still enjoyed her job and John's pit pension had started when he was 55 but he decided to carry on working until they could both retire, he had got a good lump sum and a fair pension, Grace had stopped work when she had Tony and Ellen and not returned until after the kids had been at school a few years, she wasn't due a full pension until she was sixty. They would be better off when they retired than they'd been throughout most of their married life.

John, still working but ready for retirement, was looking forward to it. They were planning to use some of the money on a good long holiday. They weren't going until after Ellen's wedding but Grace had already started dieting and she'd been bringing home brochures about cruises. It was to be the trip of a lifetime.

Ellen was planning her wedding to Mark, she'd moved back home and was saving hard for the wedding and a deposit on a house, house prices were absolutely ridiculous, £85,000 for a little old terrace. They were happy enough to start small but they were frightened of over-extending themselves. Mark had been telling her about seeing Alan last week.

Babs and Alan had got together a couple of years ago and Alan had told him how they were really struggling, they'd bought a house and had a baby, Babs had planned to stay at home until little Bobby started school but they hadn't been able to manage. Babs had just got a job on the twilight shift at a local factory, her mother had Bobby for an hour until Alan finished work. He would put him to bed before she got home. She'd only been back at work a few weeks and still felt guilty about not being there to put him to bed although she knew Alan enjoyed the time he spent with Bobby, he seemed to be always tired but fatherhood certainly had its compensations, he loved being a dad but he was worried, interest rates were going up, they'd got a fixed rate deal for two years but it was time to find a new deal and it wasn't going to be easy.

Mark had arranged with Ellen to visit them on Saturday evening, it had been ages since they'd had a night out and it wouldn't cost much. A couple of bottles of wine and a few cans should do it.

Saturday evening they went round early because Ellen wanted to see Bobby before he went to bed.

Mark and Alan sat down with drinks while Ellen and Babs put Bobby in the bath.

Bobby had enjoyed his bath but was tired and fretful while Babs was drying him and getting him ready for bed.

"I've been thinking about those discussions we used to have with your mum and dad" Babs was saying, ignoring Bobby's grumbling.

"The Great Money Trick seems more relevant now. Alan works as much overtime as he can but we're barely managing.

Do you remember that night at your parents? I struggled with it that first night when your mum tried to explain it to us but now it's so obvious—it's actually worse now than then. We don't even get to hold the money now, wages are paid direct in to the bank—standing orders, direct debits out—gas, electric, council tax, mortgage, insurance, TV licence, credit card payments—if there's any left we spend it on food and such but more often than not now there's none left by the end of the month so we have to rely on the credit card.

It should get a bit easier now I'm back at work part time but it doesn't seem right that I can't stay at home with Bobby while he's so young.

My mum enjoys having him but, as she says, she's not as young as she was and an hour or two on an evening is all she can manage.

Alan's stressing about the mortgage, I'm tired all the time and we don't seem to be able to get through a month without relying on the credit card for essentials. It's worse than your mum's old analogy of the pit village, we've been using the credit card while Alan's been working and I was getting maternity pay until I started back.

Now I think about it I can't remember feeling that much better off before I had Bobby and we were both working full time then. The mortgage is crippling us but what option did we have? We thought about renting but rents are nearly as high as the mortgage and once we'd decided we wanted to have a family as soon as possible we knew we had to get somewhere we could get settled, all we could find for rent were 6 months tenancies"

Ellen didn't know what to say, Babs looked shattered, Alan seemed quieter than usual, they'd both enjoyed the discussions when it was all theory but now Babs was suffering the consequences at what should have been the happiest time of her life. Her and Alan were so right for one another, the baby was planned, the house was an ex-council house so it was relatively cheap compared with others they'd looked at, they both worked hard. It shouldn't be like this.

They all enjoyed the night, it made a change for Ellen and Mark, they'd been staying in a lot to save for the wedding, they'd played a few games of cards got a bit tipsy, generally relaxed and on the way home they talked.

"I've got to admit it scares me a bit." Mark said "Alan's on a similar wage to me and they're really struggling, we were talking while you and Babs were putting Bobby to bed, he told me they could lose the house. Babs doesn't know how bad things are, he doesn't want to worry her but she must have some idea because she didn't argue when he suggested she go back to work."

"She knows alright and it's got me worried too. Will we be ok?

I don't really want to wait long before having a baby. We haven't really talked about it but I'll be 31 when we get married, we can't wait very long can we?"

"No but I think we need to be trying to find somewhere pretty old something we can do up as we can afford it, an old terraced or something, it's not what I planned but I don't see what else we can do."

Chapter 7

It was late August and John and Grace had just returned from two weeks in Spain with Laura and Eddy, Ellen had been waiting for them—she was bursting to talk to them.

"The kettles on, there's a nice salad in the fridge, have you seen the news while you've been away? It's really kicking off—Northern Rock has had to be bailed out by the government—there's been queues of people drawing money out, the government have promised ordinary savers won't lose their money—but the queues continued—The US sub-prime market seems to have been at the heart of the problem—selling to people who couldn't afford to buy, people with a bad credit history, at high interest, on the premise that house prices would keep going up so the banks would get their money back even if the buyers defaulted on the loans—then selling the debt on—apparently Northern Rock bought billions of pounds of the sub-prime debts then as problems in USA came to light they tried to offload it but couldn't—it seems they don't even know how much the unenforceable debt is."—She finally stopped for breath.

"We've only been to Spain not Outer Mongolia, we've been getting the English papers, a day late but we caught up on the way home so don't worry. It's going to be interesting, it could even be good news for you and Mark because house prices have been far too high for the last few years.

Our house has gone up in price 350% in the last 6 years, it's ridiculous, and the government have been trying to keep wage rises to 3%. How do they expect young people to be able to get on the housing ladder?

At least you haven't committed yourselves yet."

"Is Mark coming round later?" Grace said coming in to the living room with drinks "I've been thinking about you both. I might have a solution to your housing problem but you'd have to think it through and be sure you both agree."

"It all sounds a bit mysterious and yes he's coming round, I thought he'd be here by now" Ellen said as she heard a knock and Mark walked in "Come and sit down love, mum might have found us somewhere to live, come on mum"

"Look Mark it's only a suggestion but, before we went away my mam was saying that the house is too big for her on her own and I'm sure she'd love you two to move in with her. It's got three bedrooms and there's the little sitting room gran doesn't use, it's a good house, you could make it nice.

Obviously you'll have to think about it, talk about it, and I know it's not what you want and it's not ideal but it would be a load off my mind knowing she's not on her own."

Mark and Ellen looked at one another, too surprised at first to say anything. As usual Ellen was the first to speak.

"Well you never cease to amaze me mum. Where did that come from? Come on Mark lets go up to my room, it could work, don't look so stunned, it's only an idea."

They were upstairs for hours and just couldn't make their minds up, they both got on with Ellen's gran but it was a big step.

A few days later Ellen bumped in to Babs while out shopping so they went for a coffee, Ellen told Babs about her gran's offer.

"Gran says we'd be doing her a favour, dad is going to move her bed down in to the little sitting room anyway because she's finding it difficult to manage the stairs and social services have put a downstairs toilet and shower in so we could have the upstairs to ourselves, we'll only have to share the kitchen.

I think it's a good idea but Mark's a bit disappointed, he wanted a house of our own but seeing you two struggle had already made him realise how difficult it would be. I can't believe how much house prices have gone up in the last few years. When me and Mark first got together we could have bought a little terraced for 35 grand, now the same house is 85.

Gran is leaving the house to me and Tony anyway—she's already asked Tony what he thought and he thinks it's a great idea.

When we do inherit, which I hope is not for years yet, I love my gran, we will have the choice of selling the house and using my half of the money on a deposit or we can stay where we are and just get a mortgage to buy Tony's half. It's a lot better than getting mortgaged up to the hilt and having to rely on both wages. I'd quite like to have a baby as soon as possible. What do you think?"

"I'm green with envy, I know what Mark's worried about and it won't be easy living with your gran but what an opportunity. You could even move the wedding forward."

"I hadn't thought about that but you've helped me make my mind up. I'll talk to Mark again and if he agrees we'll start decorating straight away, we'll use the biggest bedroom as a sitting room and decorate the little room downstairs for my gran, the whole house needs doing. We could just do that and our bedroom and leave the little bedroom until after we're married. Oh I'm so excited. I'll talk to Mark first then mum and dad. I wanted a big wedding but 'our own home' is much more important. I know Mark isn't bothered about the size of the guest list. To be honest he'll probably be quite relieved, so will dad, he's been worried about his speech, it's just mum. She's already bought her hat." Ellen laughed.

Chapter 8

Grace was rushing around doing a few last minute things before setting off to pick Ellen and Mark up from the airport, her little girl a married woman, she couldn't believe how fast her life was passing.

It had been nice seeing the 'old gang' again at the wedding, they'd all made a fuss of her, promised to call round soon, it would be good. She was going to miss having Ellen at home although she hadn't seen much of her lately while her and Mark had been doing the old house up.

Emma hadn't been able to make it to the wedding but had sent a telegram from Australia, she'd emigrated last year and seemed to be happy. Tom, Mandy and new boyfriend Sam, John and Sue had got together, Paul and new partner Betty and Jane, still on her own but apparently happily so.

Paul had wanted to talk about the economic situation but he'd been drowned out by the others. "It's a wedding you idiot" Jane laughed, but she added "It's not that I'm not interested Grace, you were spot on when you said it couldn't last, that the system would inevitably fall in to a crisis, you even said banks could go bankrupt. I didn't believe you at the time but you were spot on. We should all get together again I could do with some help on understanding what's happening, what do you lot think?" They'd all agreed even Sam and Bet wanted to come, they'd heard about the discussions and of course had watched the film about the miner's strike since all the others had been in it.

Grace would have to think about it, there were far too many to fit in to her living room, maybe they were just being polite, she'd see.

Certainly the economy seemed to be in freefall she mused, banks being bailed out by the government, well by taxpayers actually, it seemed John had taken his pension just in time, the stock market had dropped with the news of the banking collapse and 'pension pots' were shrinking.

MFI had gone bankrupt, she'd not been married long when she first heard of them, they were pretty new then, she remembered, they were only doing mail order.

John had ordered some furniture from an ad in the newspaper. It had been the first new furniture they'd bought, everything they had up to that point had been second hand, the family had all rallied round when they'd got a council house only two months after they'd got wed.

Things were different now she thought, Ellen and Mark had a nice little nest egg saved, they'd decorated mam's house throughout, the kitchen was great, they'd taken advantage of the MFI closing down sale and got all the kitchen units at less than half price and even a new bathroom suite. She was glad they'd decided to move in with her mam, she hoped it would be alright, her mam was certainly happier than she'd been since dad died.

She'd even put up with all the upheaval without too much moaning and she did like the way they'd decorated the little sitting room downstairs to make a bedroom. Mark had insisted on buying her a new TV, one of those flat screen ones as a gift for putting up with the mess and the mates they'd had round most nights helping with the renovation of her house. She'd kept the old TV for her bedroom, "there's nothing wrong with it" she'd insisted, "It'll see me out".

Ellen and Mark were tired when she'd picked them up so she'd taken them straight to her mam's, she'd have to start thinking of it as theirs now she supposed.

Chapter 9

Ellen was nervous, she'd invited the whole family round for Sunday lunch and was panicking a bit. Dad had brought some extra chairs round and taken gran back to theirs until lunch was ready but Mark wasn't much use at cooking so it was all down to her. He had prepared all the veg and set the table, everything was cooking nicely but how do you get it all served up without it going cold?

She phoned her mum who was always good in a crisis "what about that lovely dinner service your gran gave you for a wedding present, I'm sure there are big serving dishes in that, just mash the spuds first then put it all in dishes and we'll help ourselves, you can leave them in the kitchen and we'll carry our plates through.

We're just setting off now and Tony's just rung to say they're on their way. It doesn't have to be ready when we arrive, we'll be there in five minutes and I'll help."

The meal was over, gran had gone for a lie down and Grace and Claire were washing up.

"It must have been a shock when you found out Woolworths was in trouble, did you know before they announced it on TV? Have you heard anything more since?" Grace asked.

"The manager called us all together before opening last week and told us there were problems nationally, sales have dropped off so profits were down. A big interest payment was due and the bank refused to extend the loan until after Christmas, I heard it was Northern Rock but it's only a rumour, it makes sense though because they've been taking a real hard line on mortgage repossessions since the government bailed them out in the summer.

It seems one of the conditions of the bail-out was that they had to repay the government as soon as possible so they appear to have stopped lending and are refusing to extend loans to help people who are struggling.

Our store is one of the best in the country, we're nearly always in the top ten for sales and have been making a profit while other bigger stores aren't but if they can't find the loan payment we're all going down.

Still its early days, the manager thinks the government might lean on the bank, we're talking about 32,000 jobs if Woollies close. It doesn't bear thinking about"

"I hadn't realised there would be so many redundancies, but you're probably right, the government can't afford to let that happen when they've just spent billions bailing out the bank. What about you? You've been there since leaving school, it wouldn't be easy getting a job so close to home. I know you'll have a good reference and with your experience you should be snapped up but there's nothing local and the whole staff looking at the same time."

"I know, we've been talking about it and Tony thinks if I do get made redundant we should buy a car with my redundancy money, we've been thinking about it anyway. The van is always full of tools so it's a major job emptying it when we go away. We will be ok anyway, don't worry about us. It might not happen and if it does it we'll deal with it, you know Tony, he is so careful, we are still looking for the 'perfect house' but if we have to stay in the flat for another couple of years it won't be the end of the world"

"Will you be ok? We'll help if you need it, you know that. Tony will be worried, he's not had much work lately has he?"

""We'll manage, as I said, we will get a car but we'll put the rest of my redundancy money away as a bit of security, I'll get a job, I can turn my hand to most things. I've been doing shop work since leaving school a change might be good for me.

I've just finished a course on office skills. I was hoping to get a transfer to a different branch because I understand one of the managers at Doncaster is retiring soon. I've worked my way up to deputy manager, I thought I was in with a chance of that job but new skills won't be wasted.

It's a bit scary but exciting too."

Two weeks later Claire found out the government would and did let Woolworths go to the wall. 32,000 people made redundant.

"Absolutely outrageous" John said when she called round the night it had been announced.

"They bailed out the fat cat bankers but let thousands of workers be thrown on the scrap heap. They are worse than the Tories. They should have nationalised Northern Rock and any other banks that want help, opened the books to find out where the money's gone and have the bank managed by a board made up of representatives from government, unions and workers that could then have made decisions based on need not greed.

No house repossessions, extensions on loans if it protected jobs, instead they spend billions of our taxes and haven't even discussed taking any control, halting repossessions or extending loans to help business.

In fact I heard earlier at work that Northern Rock has been responsible for the majority of evictions since they were bailed out. I think it's right about them being responsible for Woollies closing as well, apparently they were told to repay the bail-out money back as soon as possible so refused to extend loan payments.

It's not over yet, other business' will follow, could even see more banks in a mess. No-one knows how much the banks are involved in the toxic debts created by the sub-prime markets in America. It's going to be interesting to watch but absolute misery for millions of workers. We'll see redundancies on a massive scale, house-building will no doubt slow down now so many houses are coming on the market through evictions.

It will impact on Tony too, when people tighten their belts home improvements are the first thing they'll cut back on, it's a shame, he's been so busy lately with those housing association houses that went up near us but with all the uncertainty now no-one knows what will happen."

Chapter 10

Grace had been furious when the MP's expenses' scandal came out, as she told Ellen "I wasn't political when Thatcher came to power, I remember thinking 'well at least we might get some sensible decisions with a woman in power' it seems incredible now but I really couldn't see how politics effected me until that woman took on the miners. I remember her on the news, she talked about how bad things had got under the Labour government and how we needed pay restrain, she said she wouldn't be taking a pay increase, I actually admired her for it although I knew her pay was far more than I could ever earn, and now 25 years later I find out that MP's simply changed the way and the amount of expenses they could claim. Used expenses to pay themselves more than the pay rise they'd refused. It really makes me so angry."

Ellen was equally angry. They had a good half hour running down the MP's before Ellen got around to her news. Emma was coming home from Australia for a month and she wanted a big get-together with all her friends and family. She had specifically mentioned Grace and John so Ellen wanted to make sure they were free at the weekend.

Grace was quite excited, getting ready to go out.

Emma was home and they were having a drink in the club. The old crowd would be there, others too of course, all Emma's family would be there, she knew Emma's parents from way back.

They'd had a little van and delivered fruit and veg around the streets every week when she was first married then ran a market stall. It would be good to see them again.

It didn't take long for the talk to get around to the MP's expenses scandal.

"A floating duck house? A £9000 television? Who do they think they are? Or more important how stupid do they think we are?" Said Emma's mum. "All they say is 'we have abided by the rules' well they wrote the rules and If they haven't broken them then the rules must be wrong.

We worked all our lives and have to pay tax on our pension and they're using our taxes to fund a lavish lifestyle we will never be able to afford. It's the arrogance that gets to me. Who was the one who said 'they're only complaining because they're jealous that I live in a big house'? We're not jealous because he's got a grand house, we're bloody angry because he wants us to pay for it for him."

Everyone was furious about it, it seems to have politicised everyone.

They had a good night catching up with everyone but John was restless,

"The expenses scandal seems to have woken everyone up but what can we do about it. We need a new worker's party, someone to represent us, ordinary people. The Labour government don't even pretend any more. The cabinet are so far removed from workers they didn't even discuss bailing out Woolworth's, just a wringing of hands and stupid platitudes then even more measures to make life difficult for those on the dole. At least they have made some moves to help with home repossessions but too little too late."

Grace was more philosophical, she thought that the exposure of politicians' greed and total lack of morals was good for the argument that workers needed a new worker's party. The election was some way off but there was talks going on in unions and left groups. Maybe this would be the push needed to make it more concrete.

They talked about 'the new worker's party' for a while before bed. It was an exciting prospect.

Chapter 11

Grace was feeling a bit stunned. The new workers Party was no longer just an idea but had a name, the Trade Unionists & Socialist Coalition (TUSC) and was standing in a few parliamentary seats in the 2010 election—but the strangest thing of all was that she was the election agent for the local candidate, Bill.

There had been far ranging discussions about the new Parties programme but Grace was very pleased with the result.

Public ownership, not private profit

- Stop all privatisation, including the Private Finance Initiative (PFI) and Public-Private Partnerships (PPP). Bring privatised public services and utilities back into public ownership under democratic control.
- Keep Royal Mail as a publicly-owned service, not a privatised cash cow.

No cuts—for quality public services

- Take rail back into public ownership and build an integrated, low-pollution public transport system.
- For a high-quality, free National Health Service under democratic public ownership and control.

- Stop council estate sell-offs and build eco-friendly, affordable public housing.
- Good, free education for all, under democratic local authority control, student grants not fees.

Jobs, not handouts to the bankers and billionaires

- Bring banks and finance institutions into genuine public ownership under democratic control, instead of giving huge handouts to the very capitalists who caused the crisis.
- Tax the rich. For progressive tax on rich corporations and individuals, with a crackdown on tax avoidance.
- For massive investment in environmental projects.

Employment and Trade Union rights

- Repeal the anti-Trade Union laws.
- A minimum wage set at half average adult male earnings, with no exemptions.
- Invest to create and protect jobs, including for young people.
- Solidarity with workers taking action to defend jobs, conditions, pensions, public services and Trade Unions. Reinstate full Trade Union rights to prison officers.

Protect our environment—stop global warming

- Deep cuts in greenhouse gas emissions—otherwise climate change, caused by capitalism, will destroy us.
- Invest in publicly-owned and controlled renewable energy.
- Move to sustainable, low-pollution industry and farming—stop the pollution that is destroying our environment.
- Recognise that many of our planet's resources are limited and that capitalism fritters them away for profit.

- Produce for need, not profit, and design goods for reuse and recycling.

Decent pensions and benefits

- Restore the pre-Thatcher real value of pensions. Reinstate the link with average earnings.
- Protect entitlement to benefits, for living benefits, end child poverty.

Democracy, diversity and justice

- Welcome diversity and oppose racism, fascism and discrimination. Defend the right to asylum.
- Ensure women have genuinely equal rights and pay.
- Defend our liberties and make police and security democratically accountable.

Solidarity not war

- Bring home all British troops from Afghanistan immediately—no more wars for resources.
- No more spending on a new generation of nuclear weapons, huge aircraft carriers or irrelevant euro fighters—convert arms spending into socially useful products and services.
- An independent foreign policy, based on international solidarity—no more being a US poodle, no moves towards a capitalist, militarist United States of Europe, no Lisbon Treaty.

Socialism

- For a democratic socialist society run in the interests of the majority of people not millionaires. For bringing into democratic public ownership the major companies and banks that dominate the economy, so that production and services can be planned to meet the needs of all and to protect the environment

Bill was a member of the RMT union, he'd worked for British Rail (BR) for years then as part of the break-up of BR was transferred to Network Rail who had responsibility for maintaining the tracks then hived off to Jarvis who got the contract when it was up for tender.

Jarvis had gone in to liquidation and all the workers had been made redundant. The RMT had asked Bill to stand against Ed because he was Energy Minister and could and should have intervened to protect the workers but instead simply ignored it on the grounds that it was a private company and not government responsibility.

Ed was a Doncaster MP and much to her surprise Grace had been asked to be the agent for Bill. It was exciting but scary too.

There was only 6 weeks to the election when the decision was made to stand and no-one except members of the RMT and Left activists had heard of TUSC so she knew it would be an uphill struggle.

Bill was an excellent choice, a life-long Trade Unionist, a good speaker with an unfailing sense of humour but furious that the Labour government had allowed the break-up of British Rail and washed their hands of the outrageous sacking of his workforce.

The campaign was going well. A leaflet was to be delivered to every home through the post so their job was to get out on the streets and talk to people about the new coalition and try to convince them that a new formation had a chance to be elected or at least worth a protest vote.

They were out every day, had got good support from activists in the region as well as RMT members. They had stalls around the district with petitions in support of the Jarvis workforce and leaflets about TUSC and their socialist programme, only two weeks to go to the election now and they were preparing for a public meeting.

They'd had a good response on the streets but many, while confirming the need for a total reorganisation of the way things were done and expressing anger at the way the Labour government had let them down by supporting the banks and ignoring the people still said they would be voting Labour to keep the Tories out.

Not surprising really, the anger against the Tories was still strong in the area after the closure of the pits. Younger voters were generally disinterested in politics, lived under a Labour government most of their lives yet had watched the area go downhill throughout their lives and had seen nothing to inspire them to get interested. Most had never voted and had no intention to.

Chapter 12

The first thing they needed was some publicity. A new coalition six weeks before an election was a mad idea but they had to start somewhere. A public meeting was quickly arranged. The RMT emailed all their Doncaster members, Mark spent hours on the phone contacting anyone and everyone they collectively knew to spread the word about the meeting. Leaflets were widely distributed in the town centre. A week to organise!

Grace was pleased to see the old crowd from the Miners' Film were there as well as quite a few she didn't know.

John chaired the meeting, thanked the audience for their attendance then went on to explain the reason behind the formation of a new coalition.

Explaining how the coalition involved the RMT, the rail-workers union, the Socialist Party, the Socialist Workers Party and many individual Trade Unionists and Socialists.

Bill was the first speaker.

He started with how pleased he was to be standing for a new Party and how appropriate it was to be in Doncaster to launch TUSC, the Trade Unionist & Socialist Coalition. He thought it particularly fitting because the Labour Party had been initiated in Doncaster by three rail workers early last century and that was now so firmly committed to Capitalism that the need for a new worker's party was obvious! He went on to say,

> **There's a dire shortage of housing in Britain but there's enough bricks to build a million houses and there are thousands of bricklayers, joiners, painters, plumbers unemployed or under-employed languishing on the dole, desperate for work. Under the present system houses are not being built. Why? To keep the price of houses artificially high! The human misery of homelessness is ignored in the pursuit for more and bigger profits.**

> **Over 30,000 pensioners die of cold related illness every winter in Britain but the fuel companies are making billions of pounds profit from the outrageously high gas and electric prices. British Gas alone are expecting to make £540million profit this year, an increase of 36% and the managing director enjoys an annual salary of £1.1million. It sounds like a lottery win to me but to put it in context it's £22,000 a WEEK, not bad when pensioners have to live on £100 a week and Job Seekers allowance for the acknowledged, almost 3,000,000 unemployed (650,000 extra since the financial crisis began) is only £64.50.**

> **What's the solution? The government spent £1.2 Billion of taxpayer's (our) money bailing out the banks because they were on the point of bankruptcy but it didn't solve the crisis, in fact it added to it. 100,000 bank workers have been thrown on the dole to cut costs but the bonus system is still going on for the fat cat bosses**

On a national and international scale capitalism is out of control!

The problem of global warming will not be solved by market based ideas or technical adjustments. Solving the climate change crisis is not a technical but a political issue. We have the technology and the finances to halt and reverse the environmental crisis that is developing but we need control of the means of production to be taken by the majority instead of it resting in the hands of a privileged few. Production and trade must be planned and put under democratic control.

The Labour Party no longer represents the working class. I remember Christmas 2009 when the bankers £billions in bonus' were exposed! There was natural outrage because the banks had been responsible for the world financial crash. Labour apologists were on TV telling us that the banks had actually managed to pay back some of the money we had lent them so they had to be rewarded. Well bully for them! They borrowed money from government (us) at half a percent interest then lent it to us in loans at 14%, 15%, 24% and they make money. Wow! How could they fail? But worth a bonus? I don't think so!

There was an MP on Newsnight trying to answer the question 'Why should we pay bankers who have got us in to the financial meltdown a bonus?'

I could have felt sorry for him. He stammered and stuttered basically saying it's very complicated, there's 'derivatives' and 'futures'

and 'er derivatives and 'er other things which most people don't understand, we have to let them have good bonus' or we'll lose them to other countries. Basically saying they're cleverer than us and we just have to let them get on with it.

The MPs are all busy trying to justify the crash and justify the bonus system when they clearly don't understand how it happened but the bankers have talked a load of waffle, with great confidence and none of the MP's dare admit the truth. It's like the old children's tale the Emperor's New Clothes. If they can't understand the nonsense they are being told then they must be stupid or not fit for office.

During 13 years of a Labour government they've carried out a disgraceful social experiment that has seen their role increasingly reduced to commissioners for services delivered by the private sector.

Bill finished up with an appeal to vote for him.

Claire was next. She was nervous 'why had I offered to speak?' she asked herself, 'I'm not a public speaker, I should have left it to the others, it had seemed easy when I had been so carried away with the idea of being involved with the embryo of a new worker's party'—she felt sick with nerves then suddenly she heard John introducing her. She stood up, not looking at anyone she launched in.

"Do you know what was voted as the greatest song of the 20th century in a TV poll? It was Imagine by John Lennon. It was written in John's intensely political phase, when he marched against the Vietnam War, spoke out

against global poverty and donated money to the Upper Clyde ship-builder's 'work-in'.

The song itself evokes the vision of a socialist world, a world free from inequality, exploitation, racism and war. Imagine all the people living life in peace."

She stopped and looked around, there were some people she knew but most were strangers to her. No one was laughing, all looked interested in what she had to say! She continued.

The intellectual and moral arguments for abolishing Capitalism are simple but I want to inspire you all to get involved, not just in this election campaign but in the day to day fight to improve the lives of your families and communities, to stand up for your beliefs with conviction and courage, to explain the case to others.

We can win like we did in the anti-poll tax campaign. Ordinary people got themselves organised and fought against the combined might of the hated Thatcher government, Labour controlled councils and the courts and brought down, not only the poll tax but Thatcher herself.

Now is the time to change and transform society. It is vital for the 1.2 billion people that live in extreme poverty on less than 66 pence a day, according to the World Bank, half the world's population, 3 billion people, live on less than £1 a day, the poorest 57% of the earth's population get just 6% of the income.

Poverty, starvation, disease, pollution, racism and war stalk the planet. The gap between rich and poor grows ever wider. In Britain under a Labour government over the past 13 years the gap between rich and poor widened more than in the 18 years of Tory rule.

It might not seem like it just now but we live in an affluent society, there's plenty of money swilling around the planet. Every day £750 billion is gambled on the world stock exchanges and currency markets yet people are starving.

Under a socialist society wasteful production could be reduced and useful production increased. There are a million people in Britain on waiting lists for social housing, it would be an immediate priority of a socialist government to employ construction workers to start a massive house-building programme, to build decent affordable housing., a good, cheap, possibly free public transport system, internationally, increased agricultural production to wipe out starvation, to stop the slaughter of a baby every 5 seconds for want of basic food and clean water.

Wasteful production for the rich could be halted, for example executive jets, luxury yachts, private helicopters, mink coats, massive gas guzzling cars and other items that devour time and labour purely to enhance the rich's prestige. At the other end of the scale, quality control systems would be introduced to stop the flooding of world markets with sub-standard, cheap trashy goods which generally end up in the bin.

The environmental destruction caused by capitalism is deadly serious. Every second ten acres of rainforests disappear. That's 300 million acres every year, a land area almost as big as Scotland becomes barren. It's our planet. We have to stop this.

A socialist planned world economy could phase out fossil fuels, the biggest single cause of global warming and move towards new forms of energy such as wind, wave and solar power. Capitalism has not yet devised a method of privatising the wind or floating the sun on the stock market or selling the sea to the highest bidder.

Rejecting socialism because of the appalling track record of Stalinism is like refusing to eat mushrooms because toadstools are poisonous.

The battle between socialism and capitalism is essentially a conflict over whether the resources of the planet should be owned and controlled by a minority of people for their own benefit or used by the majority of people for the good of all.

Just imagine waking up in the morning to find you have won £2million. Then the same again the next day and the next, for ever! For 20 people in Britain this is no idle fantasy, people like the Duke of Westminster, Richard Branson and the Barclay twins Increase their fortune every day by £2million—without doing anything, not even buying a lottery ticket.

Globally Bill Gates, the richest man in the world has more personal wealth than 160 of the poorest countries. At the start of the millennium his personal fortune was calculated at £50 billion. If he earned no interest and went on the most extravagant spending spree imaginable and spent £1 million every day it would take the Microsoft boss 136 years to spend his fortune.

But do we want a fortune? A few years ago the Women's Communication Centre carried out the largest ever survey of women's opinion. Tens of thousands of women were asked the simple question 'What do you want out of life?'

A number of answers were repeated over and over again by thousands of women. They wanted clean air, a more equitable society, time to do the things they want, enough money to pay the bills, feed and clothe their children and have a decent standard of living without constantly worrying about debt. Good health, better working conditions, a shorter working week, access to education for themselves and a better education for their children, better and cheaper public transport, a decent house and garden, an end to war. The right to live their lives without being dictated to, more smiling faces. A happier world!

In the 21st century these demands are perfectly reasonable yet they appear unattainable to thousands of women in Britain. They appear unattainable because under capitalism the accountants who run the system on behalf of the rich tell us that we can't afford them.

The truth is all these things and much more can be achieved by organising society differently.

The key question to ask yourself is,

Which side am I on?
Private greed or social need?
Profits or people?
Inequality or fairness?
Hierarchy or democracy?
Capitalism or Socialism?

As John Lennon said over thirty years ago,

'Imagine all the people sharing all the world . . .

You may say I'm a dreamer but I'm not the only one

I hope someday you'll join us and the world will live as one.'

I would urge you all to join the Trade Unionists and Socialists Coalition and help us to fight for a better world."

There was a stunned silence for a few seconds then spontaneous applause.

A little group of six young people stood up and cheered. 'Count us in' they shouted. The meeting broke up in to chattering groups for a few minutes, Grace hugged Claire and the candidate stood up and shook Claire's hand.

John thanked the speakers and urged any in the audience who were interested in helping in the campaign or wanted to know more about the new formation, TUSC, to stay behind.

Amazingly only two people left and one of them passed a note to John with his name and phone number and a message to get in touch, he had a bus to catch so couldn't stay but wanted to know more and to help in the campaign.

As Claire left the stage she was immediately surrounded, the group of young people and a few others.

Grace, John, Bill and Tony spoke to little groups while Mark took names and contact numbers of people who wanted to help them campaign.

That night Grace couldn't sleep. She was excited about the response at the public meeting, thrilled that they had now 40 extra helpers to spread the word, worried about the vote which she knew would be small because hardly anyone had heard of TUSC, however good a campaign they ran they had a mountain to climb . . . . but above all else she was worried about the supporters being disappointed in a small vote.

The manifesto was excellent—not a revolutionary programme, all could be achieved under capitalism it was simply a transitional programme that would challenge the traditional Parties to decide whose side they were on.

After a fruitless hour worrying she slipped out of bed to make a cup of tea and John followed her down. He'd been kept awake by the same worries.

They talked around the subject for a while, it was John's idea that they should have an activist meeting the day before the election by way of celebration for all the work that would have gone in to the campaign but also to lay out the reasons why the vote would be low.

They finally returned to bed at about 2am but both slept easier because they'd talked it through.

Chapter 13

The campaign went well, Bill rode around the constituency on his cycle, talking to people in all the villages. They had local campaign stalls in many villages. Bill had been interviewed for local radio and had a good statement in the local press but national media totally ignored them

The support for their manifesto was great on the streets but many people raised the fear of a Conservative victory meant they felt that tactically they had to vote Labour. It was very frustrating!

After the short but exhilarating and exhausting campaign it was all over. The night before the election they met up with their supporters in a local pub. They'd all agreed to bring food and after filling their plates all settled down.

Bill stood to thank Grace for the magnificent campaign they'd had and everyone for the work that had been done. He went on to say if it hadn't been for John and Grace keeping him grounded he could have been fooled by the public response into believing that he could actually be taking office tomorrow.

Bill was a good speaker and kept them all entertained for ten minutes on his experience over the past few weeks . . . . like the day he'd been out alone on his bike, spent four hours in a local village, talking to shoppers and parents meeting their children from school. He'd had a great response but was a bit mystified that he hadn't come across anyone who'd heard of TUSC. It was only later that night when reporting back to Grace on his day that he found out the village had not been in their constituency since the last boundary change. 'Ah well' he continued to laughter 'it's a starter for the next election when TUSC will be standing in all three seats'.

Ellen got up next. She was so excited she couldn't stand still, changing from one foot to the other, her arms waving about madly. It was the first election she'd been really involved in. She'd done some leafleting in the past for the Labour Party with her parents but nothing like this!

Ellen had been most impressed with how quick witted Bill had been when very early in the campaign he'd had a telephone call local from local radio. Bill had been an active Trade Unionist all his working life but had never been active in politics. He'd agreed to stand when asked by his Trade Union and knew why we needed a Party to represent the working class but wasn't fully aware of the manifesto.

He started with the Labour government's betrayal of the Network Rail workers had been sacked because Jarvis, the private company laying the tracks had gone in to liquidation and the local MP, Ed the minster for transport had refused to intervene. Went on to say he wouldn't be taking the full MP's wage but instead would be taking the average wage of the constituency but when asked about his policies he looked a bit stunned. Ellen had been standing next to him so she quickly pointed to different parts of the leaflet.

A house-building programme first, without stopping for thought Bill explained how homelessness was at the highest level for decades because of the sell-off of council houses and the refusal of governments from Thatcher on to allow councils to build.

Good, free education for all—he attacked Labour for introducing tuition fees explained that it was depriving worker's children the right to go to university

Reverse the privatisation of the NHS, he said he would re-nationalise the hospital cleaning service that had led to dirty hospitals and the spread of MRSA and other horrendous diseases.

There was a round of applause for Bill as she finished her contribution.

Grace then ended the speeches with a full summary of the work that had been done in a few short weeks.

Every house in the constituency had received a leaflet through the post, paid for through union donations. Thousands of a second leaflet distributed by all present through door knocking and street stalls and seconded the tribute to Bill's skills and commitment to the campaign.

But then explained that the vote was unlikely to reflect the verbal response they'd all experienced during the campaign. Reminded everyone of how the last Conservative government had decimated industry starting with the steelworks then crushing the mineworkers and closing the majority of pits, brought in the hated Poll Tax, sold off council houses and generally brought down living standards for hundreds of thousands of ordinary people.

She was aware of mutterings and frowns, especially among the younger ones.

Acknowledging the terrible record of the Labour government, taking Britain into an illegal war against Iraq, doing nothing to reverse the anti Trade Union laws brought in by Thatcher, very little to improve council houses . . . . basically pandering to business and not representing the workers who put them in power she went on to say that although workers were naturally furious with the Labour Party in office the threat of the Tories regaining power would make most voters 'hold their nose' and vote Labour in spite of their disgust at the sell out . . . .

On the morning of the election Ellen and Bill rode around the constituency with a loud hailer urging a vote for TUSC the rest of the group picked voting stations to stand outside and talk to voters going in.

The count was worrying, Labour votes were piling up but hardly any for Bill. Although it was expected Grace was disappointed but glad she'd taken the opportunity to warn everyone.

When the vote was announced TUSC had come in last but Bill gave a marvellous speech castigated Miliband for the way he'd betrayed Jarvis workers and reminding him that the Labour Party had been founded by Trade Unionists and workers to represent their interests and warning him that TUSC would grow in leaps and bounds and would sweep away the Labour Party that had betrayed their roots.

He got a rousing cheer in the room and they found out later his speech had gone viral on You Tube.

The family and some of the supporters were at Grace and Johns the next day luckily because the phone rang all day with commiserations for the vote and congratulations for putting down a marker for the future but Bill's speech on you-tube brought in more phone calls than the election. They all simply took it in turns to answer, most wanted a 'quick' word with Grace so after the first 4 calls they all agreed just to take messages for her

They opted to have fish and chips for tea then settled down to discuss the national election results which had resulted in no Party getting an overall majority.

It was an unusual situation. The Conservatives had the most seats but if the Liberals teamed up with Labour who came second then they could overturn any vote in the commons.

Grace thought the Liberals would probably prop up Labour and demand a vote on proportionate representation as the price of that support, after all they had only got 6% less of the vote than Labour but had 200 less seats.

John was less convinced. Clegg, the Lib-Dem leader was very ambitious and John thought he might enter a coalition with the Tories. Nobody else could see this happening they agreed with Grace although Tony wondered about the Tories running a minority government.

It took five days for the Conservatives' and Lib-Dems to form a Coalition which disorientated many of Lib-Dem members on both sides.

Grace knew the Conservatives would use the excuse of the national debt caused by the world banking crisis of 2008/9 to make cuts in services because that had been their election mantra throughout the election . . . . totally ignoring the fact that all Parties supported the bailing out of the banks with tax-payers money.

She expected there to be a period of strikes and struggles as workers resisted. She knew the election of a Tory government was a setback for the workers but she didn't expect the coalition to last long so she determined that the task now was to build TUSC and get the name recognised by capitalising on the work they'd done in the election.

She was already planning how to get the name known before the next election. Local elections and single issue campaigns could be done in the name of TUSC.

Chapter 14

It didn't take long for the Tory colours to show through. Within a month of the election the Chief Secretary to the Treasury was forced to resign because he'd been exposed for fiddling his expenses while in opposition.

The Con-Dem coalition predictably went on the offensive and the first thing they did was increase tuition fees for university to £9000 a year. Students all over the country were furious.

In the general election the Lib-Dems had got thousands of student votes because they'd promised to abolish tuition fees. Clegg thought it was a good deal because the students didn't start paying it until after they'd got a job.

He'd been born to rich parents as had most of the cabinet, no idea of the misery of debt, no idea how terrifying the thought of leaving university with a debt of £27,000 just for fees added to the student loans to eat and pay rent. He'd lost all credibility when he'd sold out the students for a taste of power.

In Graces opinion it would mean their death knell. They would be consigned to the wilderness.

There were student demonstrations around the country throughout November and December 2010, the 30 to 50,000 students marched through London on the first demonstration. The police had come down hard on the students, sometimes kettling them for hours, created a lot of anger which accumulated in clashes with the police. The worst being on the day the vote was before Parliament. The vote was carried. Students were furious!

Not unexpectedly the press ignored the marvellous demonstration and instead they'd managed to find a couple of clashes with the police to report on from much smaller demonstrations elsewhere.

How could young working class youth afford to take on a £27,000 debt for a degree? She was selfishly pleased that her two were passed that stage, there was no way they could have afforded that.

The government took no heed of the protests and continued with their cuts programme, making thousands of public sector workers redundant and announced plans to cut to public sector pensions . . . . on the grounds that private workers pensions had dropped drastically and 'we're all in this together'

The TUC organised a march through central London in March 2011 in protest against public sector cuts. Over half a million Trade Unionists marched.

All the family went on the demonstration. It was great. Trade Union leaders rallied for a fight-back against these attacks on the public sector but John was sceptical.

A one day general strike would be a good starting point but he knew the Trade Union leaders were cowed by the Tory victory. The Labour Party weren't even trying to defend their record in office so although the working class were ready the leadership wasn't. The TUC had only organised the demonstration to allow workers to let off a bit of steam.

Around the country there were further demonstrations as councils set their budget, announcing great swathes of workers being made redundant. Labour councils just blamed the government instead of fighting back. Doncaster was in a worse position that most, they had a Labour council and a right wing English Democrat elected mayor.

The TUSC name was being recognised because their banner appeared on every demonstration but she knew more was needed.

Chapter 15

2012 New Years Eve and Grace was reflecting on the past year, Tony and Ellen were both settled and Ellen and Mark were talking about starting a family. She didn't think Tony and Claire would wait much longer either.

Three years into the coalition government and things were so much worse than Grace had imagined possible.

The government and media gave off a constant stream of panic statements about the dire state of the economy, how 'we're all in it together'. 'Hard decisions must be made to clear up the mess left by Labour.'

The Con-Dems had introduced a divisive language to attack the benefit system for being too generous, talking about strivers and skivers and people languishing on sickness benefit instead of getting a job. Attacks on disabled people had increased, sick people were being found fit for work and losing their benefit.

The Labour leader, Ed, the Doncaster MP who'd won the election when Bill stood for TUSC, joined in the rhetoric claiming he would be tougher on benefit scroungers, would look after the strivers! Grace was furious.

People were dying while waiting to appeal a decision that they were fit for work, people had killed themselves because they simply couldn't cope with an appeal.

Still the year had its highlights she thought

In November about 2 million public sector workers had taken strike action, teachers, probation officers, border agency staff, librarians, radiographers, social workers, court staff, refuse collectors, midwives, road sweepers, cleaners, school meals staff, tax inspectors, paramedics, customs officers, passport office staff, Jobcentre staff, civilian police staff, driving test examiners, patent office staff, health & safety inspectors . . . . the list was endless. It was magnificent.

There were over 1000 demonstrations around the country. Thousands of workers were taking action for the first time. There was a real mood to take on the government. So much anger!

The organised working class were on the move. The whole family had been on the demonstration in Doncaster. The mood was electric.

But by Christmas UNISON members had been sold out by their leadership who'd accepted a cobbled together agreement with very few concessions. Workers were furious but felt powerless at this betrayal.

Food-banks were springing up all over Britain, 3 in Doncaster already, workers and students had tried valiantly to halt the government juggernaut but Labour were backing the government in the need for a reduction in social spending and with a few notable great exceptions the TU leaders were keeping quiet as their members terms and conditions were decimated.

Sick, disabled and even terminally ill people were being found fit for work or well enough to start training to return to work. Job-seekers were being sanctioned for the tiniest mistake like being a minute late for an appointment,.

Grace just couldn't believe how much misery the government had managed to inflict in less than three years.

Still another year tomorrow she thought, time to get ready. It would be good to see the old crowd again they were all coming tonight to celebrate the end of the old year and to let in the new.

She'd been baking for days, time to relax.

By 8.30 the house was full to bursting. Grace had been pleased that Babs and Alan had come. They were staying the night in Ellen's old room and Bobby was already asleep in Tony's

Mandy had brought ingredients for a punch that she promised had a big 'kick' so urged caution to Sam and Paul who were fond of a drink, and she'd brought Elaine who she'd got friendly with after the first public meeting of Bill's election campaign. Everyone picked up a drink and scattered about the room, extended with the addition of a conservatory.

John was pleasantly surprised when Ellen started chanting speech, speech . . . . the others joined in looking at him.

He laughed self-consciously took a deep breath . . . .

> **The Con-Dem government without any opposition from Labour is waging an unprecedented attack on the living standards of a whole generation, criminalising the young, the unemployed, the poor.**
>
> **Vicious, degrading and deadly attacks on sick, disabled and the terminally ill. The welfare**

state is being dismantled at breathless speed. The health service is being overloaded with paperwork and starved of funds and the TUC are simply ignoring it.

They are scrapping Legal Aid and bringing in a Bedroom Tax.

He could feel himself getting in to rant mode

Suddenly he realised it was New Years Eve, laughing he shouted 'I think it's time we had a revolution!' he punched the air and sat down.

Grace and John moved between the groups that formed, John was interested in what Elaine was saying so he stopped for a chat. Elaine worked at the Citizens Advice as and was talking about the kind of issues that people sought advice on.

'Not surprising really that debt is a big issue' she was saying 'but what shocked me most was homelessness and the amount of substandard private rented in the area. It's difficult to advise on repairs in private rented because, although the law is very clear on the landlords responsibility and how they can be forced to carry out repairs we always have to urge caution because most tenants have short tenancy agreements so if they upset their landlord he can simply refuse to extend their tenancy.

It's very frustrating!' She said 'We need a massive house-building programme There's 11,000 people on the waiting list for social housing in Doncaster and the council I understand are not allowed to build'.

Babs, who'd been quiet up to that point, came in quite loudly with 'It's not much easier when you are buying. We only took on a mortgage because of the high rents and lack of security with 6 months contracts but we're really struggling with the mortgage since I had to give up full time work when we had

Bobby. Alan hasn't had a pay rise for 4 years and with inflation we're not really managing.

Elaine moved next to her and said quietly 'Give me a ring after the holidays and I'll do a benefit check, you might be entitled to some benefits' she handed Babs a note of her telephone number.

John jumped in to change the subject to give Babs time to recover. She looked like she was regretting her out-burst.

He asked Elaine how long she'd been working at the CAB. She looked relieved for a change of subject. It was New Years Eve after all!

Not many knew Elaine so she told them she'd been working in Woolworths when it closed down. She couldn't find work at first so she'd trained as a volunteer with CAB and was lucky enough after just over a year to get paid work there. She was an administrator three days but worked two days as a volunteer advising.

John moved off to and found Ellen waxing lyrical about her garden, she really had transformed it. She'd kept the little front lawn but had turned the rest into a super vegetable plot, they were almost self sufficient and plenty to share with the family. She was right to be proud of it he thought but he didn't stay long he found Grace to tell her about Babs and suggest she had a word to her in the morning.

As the drink flowed the talk got lighter and as midnight approached they were all sprawled across the living room listening to Mark playing old songs on his guitar with all singing the ones they knew.

What would 2013 bring?

Chapter 16

'Well who'd have thought it, standing for mayor of Doncaster as a TUSC candidate?' Grace was preparing for a local 'Question Time' with other candidates that had been organized by the local business community.

She was looking forward to it, the campaign had gone really well. They'd had meetings in 4 villages, petitioned against council cuts in others, canvassed for votes in as many areas as possible even joined social media through face-book. Every house in the district had seen the manifesto. She was very proud to be standing and was getting quite a following. Had to give an opinion on everything from resources for injured service personnel to whether Doncaster needed another gypsy and traveller site.

A program of no cuts to services and a massive house-building program which would not only create the homes desperately needed by the 11,000 people on the waiting list in Doncaster but would create jobs and apprenticeships. It would put money in pockets that would be spent which would mean more shops more goods needed. It would help to replace some of the jobs lost with the closure of most of the Doncaster coalfield.

The house-building to be funded from the capital receipts from the sale of council houses over the past 30 years. This money had been ring-fenced by Thatcher and still tied up despite 12 years of a Labour government. The only change Labour had allowed was that the accumulated interest could be used to modernise existing council housing.

Even that had led to one of the Labour councillors using the program to secure an expenses paid trip to China Grace remembered from her time in the Labour Party. Sickening!

Re-introduce the EMA (Education Maintenance Allowance) to 17 & 18 year olds to encourage them to stay in education. Almost a million unemployed young people nationally, thousands in Doncaster. Well EMA together with the creation of apprenticeships and jobs will both help to address that.

Subsidised bus fares to discourage cars, It has cost more to constantly repair the crumbling roads than was saved when the subsidies had been stopped under Thatcher.

She was looking forward to the chance to lay out their policies although realistically she didn't expect to win many votes from the business community. It would be good experience and it turned out to be just that.

Grace couldn't wait to get to her branch meeting after the forum, she'd thoroughly enjoyed it, they'd all had the opportunity to answer each question . . . . . but the National Front candidates had caused mayhem with one of his answers.

Grace initially told about sitting down next to a youngish man who backed off when she introduced herself as the TUSC candidate, he'd obviously heard that there were candidates from the far Right and far Left and introduced himself as the Conservative agent (making it sound like an apology) but settled down once he knew she wasn't going to attack him.

The questions had been as expected from business,

How to cut unemployment? With answers ranging from training programs while unemployed to one candidate promising to use part of the opulent salary the post offered to pay an apprentice to setting up apprenticeships in the council to Grace's house-building program . . . . .to the NF candidate announcing 'get rid of all the foreigners because the government pay a subsidy to employ Eastern Europeans instead of locals . . . . .quite divorced from reality that man!

How to make the airport more useful to business? Most agreed the road system to the airport needed improvement . . . . . . The NF candidate said he would turn the airport into a sports centre because if we kept the airport then foreigners would continue to come to Doncaster!

How to improve the failed services in Doncaster? Grace had jumped in on this question to announce if elected she would certainly not be handing them over to the private sector to turn the motive into profit instead of care. She'd been pleased it had given her the opportunity to expose the present mayor and the Labour council for privatizing the care of vulnerable adults in Doncaster, knowing the service would not be as good but to save 0.4%.

Someone then asked a supplementary question on how the new mayor would protect vulnerable adults after privatization?

No-one could believe it when the man from the NF had stood up to announce the only reason there were so many vulnerable adults now is that the government are injecting our children with the 'monkey gene'. Unbelievable! There had been so much understandable anger from the audience and the rest of the panel that the chair called an end to the meeting.

It had been an experience and caused much amusement when recounted in the branch meeting.

The few short weeks flew by and on the eve of the election they were having a quick last meeting of all who'd helped in the campaign.

John wanted a word about the campaign. He quickly ran through the work they'd done and the great reception they'd found for their message. How many had filled in postcards to find out more about the Socialist Party and TUSC.

He introduced a couple who'd only recently started helping since speaking to a canvasser. He congratulated them all but urged caution with expectation.

Most of them were new to politics so he explained the particular aspects of this election was the present mayor, Peter had a lot of support, he appealed to a certain section of Doncaster with his statements about 'bringing young people in control', trying to block funding for Doncaster Pride. The Labour Party had lost a lot of respect in the area but old loyalties die hard . . . . and their main message on the streets was 'if you don't vote Labour then you will let Peter back in'.

The TUSC vote will have been squeezed between the two, many people who support our ideas will hold their nose and vote Labour.

We've already succeeded in putting a Socialist programme on the agenda. I'm hoping for 1500. 1500 who have heard and responded to the programme but we won't win and more than likely will come in last.

No-one spoke for a minute till Grace shouted out 'I want 2000 votes' and every-one started laughing

Election day—Finally the campaigning was over. The vote was being counted. Everyone was nervous. They'd had a great campaign but it was important that they got a respectable vote. It was the first time a socialist option had been placed before the whole electorate. Winning was not possible so early in their existence as an electoral force. They'd had very little media coverage but all knew they'd done all they could.

Almost 2000 votes for socialism! Brilliant result! It was the main story on the official TUSC web-site and even more important new members had been won to their cause. She'd beaten the Lib-Dems and an independent.

The main task for the next period was educating new members and watching how the new Labour mayor and council would manage the council under the constraints imposed by the Con-Dem government.

Chapter 17

Time was flying by, Grace was so busy, discussing with new members, regular activities which gave the Party opportunity to talk to people on the street. The bedroom tax was causing misery for people

This vicious government had certainly politicised people but the Labour council meekly implementing them was causing anger on the streets, everyone had a story to tell.

One woman that John had been talking to last week had left a violent partner and moved to the area to escape. The police had made her 3 bed-roomed council house secure, locks and bolts, bars on the windows, fireproofed letterbox. It had cost thousands but the council said she had to move to a smaller house as her 2 children could share a room. Both children had lived through the nightmare of seeing violence, the oldest still had disturbed nights.

A man, who'd lived with his mother all his life, succeeded the tenancy to the three bedroom house. He was told if he didn't agree to move to a flat he would have to pay for the two spare bedrooms. It was his home.

A woman who's son had died she was told to give up her family home because her late son's bedroom was now 'spare'.

The worst for Grace was the very ill and disabled people who contacted her who had a separate bedroom from their partners because of their health problems and were being told to pay for a spare bedroom or move to a one bedroom property.

Grace was busy writing letters of appeal and filling in forms for Discretionary Housing Benefit to cover the bedroom tax.

The flawed decisions on fitness for work were getting worse and a national campaign had been set up against the private company who were being paid millions to carry out the 'medical' assessments.

Mass protests against all the medical centres were being planned for early in the New Year.

Grace made a mental note to find out who would be organising the local protest she couldn't find time to help with the organising because she was busy but she knew nearer time she could help ensure word went out to make it a success.

On 27th December Grace got a surprise call from a friend, Mel, she hadn't seen for twenty years. A former miner who had set up a facebook page to commemorate the 30th anniversary of the miners' strike. Grace immediately offered to help, this was something she could do at home and could be fun.

She'd started using social media during the elections and had now used it to wind down at night. She had found it a good source of information, politics and fun. As well s her personal page she posted on SP and TUSC pages.

The 30th anniversary of the miners strike was so important politically that she wanted to be part of ensuring the lessons of the miners strike were passed on to a new generation.

She looked at the page and was pleased with the blurb

'This page has been created to spread the word and re-spark the flame created by the heroic struggle of the miners in the great strike of 1984-85'

The page really took off, former miners, their families, some existing miners and many who were too young to remember the strike. Grace spent many hours over the holiday period on the page, hundreds of pictures from the strike, union banners, badges and memorabilia were sent every day.

Locally Grace and John got involved with the organising of a celebration to mark 30 years since the strike began, it was great to see old friends, one of the organisers had moved hundreds of miles away but returned for the planning meetings. He'd managed to get a grant to have a new banner made which they decided to use to celebrate women's role in the strike.

The former NHS workers had been moved over to the private sector 3 months before Christmas had just been told their wages needed to be reduced because of according to the employer 'council budget cuts' which was ridiculous. Their bid had gone in to the council and been agreed 12 months before. The workers were furious, they were expected to take a 30% pay cut.

One of the Socialist Party members was the union steward, he reported the results of the strike ballot, 97% in favour, his work colleagues were not political activists just workers who cared about their clients and fearing for their safety because of the reduced cover that would be available if the employer got away with these cuts.

The whole branch got behind the strikers and had rallies and petitioned for the contract to be returned to the health service to protect the service users as well as protect their own terms and conditions.

Chapter 18

The local demonstration against Atos was great. Grace had got involved in Doncaster after an appeal went out on social media for help to organise, one woman had been struggling alone and started to panic as the time got closer. The national organisers had suggested the demonstrations should be outside the medical centres used by the company running the 'work capability' test designed to find people fit for work.

About 30 hardy activists started the day off at 8am and gradually throughout the day we were joined by scores of others, a guy called Gordon came along just to make sure we all had hot drinks and food, greatly appreciated it was too. A film crew dropped by to interview and film the protest for a film called Return to Doncatraz.

Grace had agreed to be one of the speakers on the day and she'd been horrified when she read some of the stories of vulnerable people who'd been found fit for work.

The home made placards were brilliant 'ATOS DONT GIVE A TOSS' 'CUTTING BENEFIT ONE DEATH AT A TIME' 'CUT BANKERS BONUS NOT PEOPLES BENEFIT'

Grace was the first speaker,

The safety net of benefits has been eroded so fast under this unelected government that it has stunned people.

Lies and distortion about the benefit bill, the demonization of disabled, sick and unemployed, getting rid of Legal Aid, reduced funding for advice agencies, introduction of the bedroom tax . . . . an avalanche of misery on the most vulnerable and isolated.

A few facts that are hidden by the government and their lackeys in the media need shouting from the rooftops.

The biggest part of the benefit bill is paid to pensioners who have worked and paid their taxes and National Insurance. Next highest is low waged workers needing Tax Credits to supplement their wages then sick and disabled. The smallest group is the unemployed

The cost of living has increased 25% since the world economic crash and neither pay nor benefits have kept up with inflation, the vast majority of us have taken an effective pay cut

13million people are living in poverty in Britain the 7th richest country in the world. 3.5 million of them children, 1.5 million pensioners.

Low pay, zero hours contracts, under-employment, the slave labour scheme, workfare are a big cause of poverty in Britain but the government benefit sanctions coupled with the work capability assessment test and subsequent fitness for work decisions are causing the most misery.

She asked if others wanted to speak, one man spoke of a friend of his,

A local man, suffering anxiety and depression found fit for work the letter from the DWP said he scored no points, he didn't know what to do . . . . he killed himself.

A very articulate woman in a wheelchair with severe breathing difficulties had been put on the work related group, she explained the mental torture she was subjected to by the staff at the E4S training that she had to attend . . . . She was struggling to breath one day on her way in and one of the staff told her to get a move on in adding 'if you had learnt to read and add up at school you wouldn't be here! Her answer was 'well no-one pointed that out to me when I got my degree'.

Another told me of a workfare programme she was forced to attend, working in a warehouse, the place was infested with mice, health & safety non-existent, a pile of boxes fell on her, knocking her down, she was bruised and shaken, her boss shouted at her 'get them all stacked up again before you return to your job' . . . . this for no pay. She complained to E4S advisor and said she couldn't possibly go back there, she was crying and distraught. She was told 'you work to the end of the placement or lose your benefit' she had no option but to return or starve.

The assessment centre was situated next to the job centre and many claimants joined the demo after signing on, many had stories to tell, generally people who had been sanctioned,

One man had arrived ten minutes early, obvious to everyone that he was vulnerable, he explained he was classed as a 'slow learner' at school but had been found fit for work and forced to sign on for JSA, the security guard wouldn't let him in, he hadn't a watch so waited what he thought was sufficient time and tried again . . . . he was sanctioned for being two minutes late.

Another who had a deep scar on his skull from a motorbike accident a few years previously. The brain damage he'd suffered had affected his concentration and memory he'd been sanctioned for being late for an appointment because his bus had been delayed through a serious accident blocking the road, no benefit for two weeks. He was lucky he had family who helped him out with food and put some money on his electric card.

A woman in a wheelchair who'd had to get a lift to attend for her first JSA appointment was turned away because first appointments were not carried out on the ground floor and there was no lift.

Another woman, almost blind and waiting to go to hospital to have cataracts removed had been found fit for work and had been told to sign on for Job Seekers Allowance. Elaine advised her of the appeal process and helped her complete the form, explaining once it was received by the DWP she would be put back on sickness benefit until the appeal was heard. She advised the woman to go to her local CAB for help with preparing for the tribunal.

Ellen finished off the speeches. Grace didn't remember seeing her quite so angry as she was that day and did wonder how she could follow the real tales of misery they had been listening to but Ellen surprised her because instead of continuing with 'more of the same' she ended the day on a positive note,

> **People are getting organised, UNITE are recruiting sick, pensioners and unemployed to Unite Community for a co-ordinated fight-back . . . . but we need to unite the struggles of claimants to the fire-fighters, teachers, lecturers, civil servants and other workers and demand the TUC name the day for a one day general strike as the first move to stop these attacks and threaten more to follow. We need to**

show this government and any future Labour government that we are not prepared to pay for the financial crisis caused by the bankers 'I think it's spelt with a b'

she ended to loud applause.

Chapter 19

The Party had decided to stand in as many seats as possible in the local elections with the intention of standing enough candidates nationally, 625, to warrant a TV broadcast for TUSC. There was such a need for an alternative to austerity but they were facing a media block on their voice.

The media were falling over themselves to push a racist right wing alternative, Ukip who put the blame for the country's economic problems on the European Union and immigrants, unfortunately it was getting an echo with people who were sick of the main Parties who all agreed that 'difficult decisions were needed' which invariable meant more cuts in services and living standards for the majority.

Grace was pleased that TUSC in Doncaster had 11 candidates standing locally, one of the striking care workers and the husband of another had joined them in the electoral elections. It was their biggest electoral challenge both locally and nationally but they failed to find enough candidates to get the broadcast.

The Green Party also stood in many seats and they had agreed not to split the Left vote by standing against one another so there was a Left alternative in most seats.

Campaigning for the election passed in a blur, each candidate being responsible for getting their own leaflet out but Graces mother was getting increasingly infirm so Grace had to call on others to help her as she cared for her mother, Ellen was a great help of course

Election day seemed to come too fast and the results were quite shocking for them all. TUSC results were good, getting 1556 across Doncaster and almost 10,000 across the region but Ukip's were better, they were very close to winning every seat from Labour. They did only get one councillor elected but Labour had been forced to hold an impromptu meeting at the back of the hall to discuss what to say if Ukip took all their seats. After the results many Labour candidates thanked us for offering an alternative which they accepted had stopped Ukip from wiping them out.

Ukip's leader was naturally pleased with the results in Doncaster it was their first serious challenge to Labour and their results were outstanding in a former Labour stronghold. He announced they would be holding their annual conference in Doncaster, on the Labour leader's doorstep.

At the social that night all were talking about the threat of Ukip while they got settled. After Grace had summarised their results, announced the fantastic regional results and thanked everyone for their hard work John stood up to speak.

'I know this is a social' he said grinning but I'd just like a quick word before we get stuck in to frivolity and fun. Everyone groaned but urged him on when he made to sit down with his hands up in surrender

It's about the Ukip vote.

It is a serious threat, it's not surprising because of the media cover they've had but we need to recognise the vacuum on the Left that is

allowing their racist propaganda to sway people. It's no accident that the media hang on every word they say, my theory is that the ruling class have realised this government won't get in office again because of the devastation they were causing, in the health service, council services, schools, thousands of workers thrown on the scrap heap. The rise of deaths of claimants found fit for work, food banks, malnutrition . . . .

So they are pushing this clown and his populist policies and they have the mainstream media under their control. We need to get TUSC into the workers consciousness. Let them know our programme, see the alternative, see it doesn't have to be like this. I'm not so good at it but Grace has convinced me facebook is a powerful tool and I do realise that I'm probably the only one here who doesn't spend time on it every day but I've watched the growth of the 30th anniversary page and appreciate its potential so I think we could it to organise to get TUSC out there.

Ukip are having their conference here in Doncaster in September, there was a gasp in the room and a quick buzz of whispering. We have to organise against them. This is too serious to ignore. We need to get together with the rest of the Left and organise a grand reception for them . . . .

Now it is party time he announced as he sat down.

Chapter 20

A food bank had been set up in the village, both Grace and Elaine were helping out, people's generosity was heart-warming. A friend of John's had put a message on facebook stating there were people going hungry in our area and he wanted help to get it going . . . . Grace offered to help

He'd a great response, the Town Council let them use a community centre, the local supermarket let them stand in the supermarket for people to donate food while they were shopping. Local businesses offered fruit and vegetables, a local chip shop offered a sack of potatoes as often as we needed. In no time at all it was up and running.

When people first came in they were very generally hesitant and embarrassed but it was a warm and friendly atmosphere. Cup of tea and a biscuit, register and explain 'why the need' then they were given a bag of fruit and vegetables. Elaine offered advice if it was a benefit issue, just an overview of what steps they needed to take then pointed them to CAB if it was complicated or they needed more than initial advice.

Everyone had a story to tell but the main problem was benefit hold ups, being found fit for work and having no money until the appeal had been accepted and Job Seekers Allowance sanctions. Two men who started to come regular were well known drinkers and there was some muttering about them but Elaine, generally not one to speak out pointed out that the men hadn't started drinking to take advantage of the foodbank, fact was they had been drinking for years, the food they got from there would possibly stop them from getting malnutrition and 'that's why we set this up surely! There was stunned silence for a minute then Grace and two others clapped.

Donations of food were still coming in within months they had to start looking for some storage space. Everyone was storing food at home then bringing it in but it was not ideal.

Politically things were happening, the public sector were balloting for strike action, Grace was still working on the 30th Anniversary Page and more rallies and marches were happening all over to commemorate the strike

Around the anniversary of the strike under the 30 year rule cabinet papers were opened and many of the lies that were told in 1984 were exposed. Margaret Thatcher had constantly stated the strike was nothing to do with her or her government. She had not only been involved in running the strike she had micro-managed it. On a note she'd made, hand written, she had worked out how many lorries would need to go to the power stations to protect the supply.

Arthur, the leader of the mineworkers had said the Coal Board planned to shut 70 pits, this was denied, now we all know it was 74.

The page was so busy now, dozens of posts a day, pictures, stories, poems . . . . memories, They were advertising the rallies for the strike, building support for the strikers.

Ellen led a discussion at their weekly meeting. There were new members there she started with a bit about the Party and the socialist programme explaining that they had weekly discussions to raise their understanding and share their knowledge because all the other Parties were intent on carrying on with the austerity programme.

> **Its 30 years since the miner's strike. Thatcher and her henchmen in the government had been determined to crush the biggest, strongest Trade Union in the country. The police, courts, M15 and even social security (benefits) were used to starve the miners back to work.**
>
> **All involved knew at the time that it was a battle we could not afford to lose. It was unthinkable!**
>
> **But lose we did and since then successive governments have continued the work started by Thatcher to take back all the gains fought for by workers.**
>
> **A Poverty and Exclusion project carried out jointly by 8 universities and two research agencies have just published their findings from the biggest study ever undertaken. It makes grim reading of increased inequality and poverty in the UK.**
>
> **A few figures first but don't worry about remembering them I've got copies. She said waving her notes in the air.**
>
> **Numbers living in poverty have more than doubled to 33% in the 30 years since the miner's strike.**
>
> **18 million people cannot afford adequate housing, 2.5 million children live in damp homes, 1.5 million children live in cold homes, 4 million children and adults are not properly fed.**

1 in 3 cannot afford to heat their homes in winter, 1 in 4 consider themselves to be poor, 17% of adults in paid work are defined as poor and 21% in arrears on essential household bills.

It is an outrage that in one of the richest countries in the world there is so much poverty, desperation and misery.

It's not all bad news of course £billions are being handed over to a few fat cats companies to throw sick, disabled and dying people off benefits, £billions to companies to privatise chunks of the NHS, £8 billion I think it was in tax cuts to the richest.

The chancellor tells us his policies are working, we are coming out of recession? He must be talking about the fat cats he's certainly not talking about the thousands suffering malnutrition in Britain, he's certainly not talking about the massive national debt left over from the bail-out of the banks and he cannot be talking about borrowing being down because this government have borrowed more in 4 years than the previous Labour government did in 12!

Maybe he's just LYING again!

We need a united working class fight-back against the whole austerity package on offer from the 3 main parties and the racist populist Ukip.

Some of the biggest Trade Unions have or are balloting for joint strike action on 10th July. The

NUT, PCS, UNISON, UNITE and others. This could be bigger than the 1926 General strike.

The TUC have failed to move on the mandate for a general strike, it looks like workers are taking it in to their own hands now. This is a battle we cannot afford to lose!

One of the newcomers was a teacher so he told us of the activity that had been planned so far for the strike day. Two UNISON stewards from health and a Care UK worker added their plans. It was going to be an impressive turn out.

Grace and Elaine still helped out at the foodbank once a week. It had a facebook page and Elaine put a piece in about the people who helped and used the foodbank.

The foodbank has been open less than 9 months but the difference it has made to vulnerable local people is immeasurable.

150 people have registered and have accessed it 561 times.

Everyone who needs it gets a bag of basic food, tins, rice, pasta etc and a bag of fruit and vegetables. We have recently managed to get a regular supply of bread too.

1112 bags of food have been given out, an incredible 4 Tons.

None of this would be possible without the great folk of the area who have given massive support to fill the desperate need for the most basic of needs—FOOD.

We've got an allotment so next year will have a supply of 'home grown' fresh vegetables to supplement the ones kindly provided by local business

The volunteers have very varied backgrounds and life experience but have become a group of close friends over the past few months.

To give you an idea of the kind of people who have been forced into this situation by the low wage economy and vicious cuts to the benefit system and sanction regime (benefits stopped for fictitious or miniscule infringements of the rules),

63 on sick, 49 signing on for JSA, 7 OAP and 14 working plus 31 on absolutely no income through sanctions.

119 children do not have to go to bed hungry because of the sterling work of the volunteers and supporters. Thank you all.

Within six months a local sports club offered the use of their club and let them shelve out a big lock up cupboard, the length of the kitchen. This was much better, more comfortable, small tables and chairs set out so people could talk privately. They'd even set up an outreach close to the community centre for people who found it more difficult to get to the club. Some folk who came for food during an emergency returned to help out or sometimes to bring food and have a coffee.

The community spirit which Thatcher and her henchmen had tried to crush was alive and well she told John after returning home one day. She had been moved by a young woman who'd called in that morning with her mother. They didn't want food they had heard that they could get some advice.

Elaine was busy seeing someone else so Grace sat with them. The young woman had had cancer for three years, she was quite ill and waiting to go back into hospital for another round of treatment but wanted advice because twice she'd had her sickness benefit stopped and had successfully appealed but she was due to go for another medical and wanted to know if she could get any help if she was found fit for work again. She said she was constantly tired and just wasn't well enough to keep battling.

She had a 6 year old and her mother had moved in with them to look after her daughter and grandchild.

Grace couldn't get them out of her mind. Elaine had told her afterwards that she had been able to help and had made sent them to the CAB for more detailed help, Elaine didn't talk about people who she spoke to there but because they had talked to Grace first she let Grace know they were helped.

Not for the first time Grace wondered how she'd ever found time to work, it reminded her a bit of the strike, always someone to see something to do but she loved it.

Chapter 21

The Ukip conference was fast approaching, most of the Left groups were involved. They'd had a great response from the Trade Unions, many were sending coaches. They'd had Saturday stalls petitioning against Ukip and building for the turn-out. They'd organised activities at one of the pubs for children and people who couldn't follow the march.

Socialists from all over Yorkshire and beyond came up for the day to show Ukip they weren't wanted here.

A few EDL and BNP supporters along with some mindless morons turned up but were obviously stunned at the size of the march so just stayed near the police and shouted at the marchers from corners. Pathetic!

On the day it was a great atmosphere, the, biggest march in Doncaster for years possibly ever.

The police were friendly and helpful, bit unnerving really said John afterwards. He had never got over the way they had treated the miners in 84/5.

Other expressions of working class anger at the Con-Dems were taking place around the country

In October around 100,000 Trade Unionists and supporters attended the TUC's 'Britain Needs A Pay Rise' demonstration in London.

Trade Unionists from every union lined the embankment to march to Hyde Park for a rally against the cuts in living standards through an average of £50 a week in the value of average wages since the financial economic crash in 2007.

At the rally speaker after speaker condemned the attacks on workers in both the public and private sector but only the general secretary of the public sector union PCS called for a national Trade Union organised one day general strike as a starter to end the massive onslaught on jobs and essential services

The mood of the rally was brilliant but it wasn't enough to stop the austerity onslaught. Direct action was needed. A mass rally was simply the TUC method of posturing to allow workers to let off steam while ignoring the demand for a general strike.

Grace was getting increasingly angry at the misery being inflicted by the government but even angrier at the cowardice of the Labour leadership in refusing to challenge the government in there being a need for austerity at all. She had just read the Joseph Rowntree Trust year-end report and it made for grim reading. Nothing she didn't know already but they were useful statistics for the member to know.

That night at the meeting Elaine was leading off a discussion on benefit cuts so Grace sent her a link to the report.

Elaine was a bit nervous but told Grace the report had been useful and she'd included some of the facts. Once she started though her nerves vanished. She was passionate about changing society, she worked at the CAB and dealt with the misery being inflicted on people on a daily basis.

I'm struggling to understand what's happening in society today. A few years ago I remember moaning about how bad things were and Grace told me how things had deteriorated since the miners' strike.

I could not remember a time of full employment and remember thinking how strange it would be to experience, live through, such changes in life.

Well I know now! From a World Economic Crash, the Greek Economy bankrupt, Italy, Spain, Ireland struggling to survive. Closer to home malnutrition at levels not seen since the end of the Second World War.

Now we have the government telling us that the economy has picked up, deficit slowing, employment up, more businesses started.

I know unemployment figures are down but that's because of 900,000 sanctioned, a million on workfare and thousands doing part-time self employed work to claim tax credits instead of Job Seekers Allowance.

The chancellor tells us his policies are working, we are coming out of recession? He must be talking about the fat cats he's certainly not talking about the thousands suffering malnutrition in Britain, he's certainly not talking about the massive national debt left over from the bail-out of the banks and he cannot be talking about borrowing being down because this government have borrowed more in 4 years than the previous Labour government did in 12 years!

> **Its time for the Trade Unions to get together and
> organise a real fight back. A one day general
> strike would be a good starting point'.**

The discussion that followed was lively, members were angry
about the lies that were constantly being told by government
but the most annoying aspect was the way the Labour MP's
were not exposing them.

John pointed out that if elected the Labour Party had said they
would stick to Tory spending plans. But bring in a mansion
tax and fund the health service with the money. They had also
said they would build 200,000 houses but since they wouldn't
explain where the money was coming from it wasn't believed.

When the meeting got to the last item on the agenda, any other
business, one of the newer members George said he had been
listening to an Italian radio program, a story about Iceland's
on-going revolution—'it is stunning how the Icelandic people
have changed their country and even more notable how quiet
our media are about this challenge to the capitalist system.

He reminded the members that at the start of the 2008 financial
crisis, Iceland had literally gone bankrupt. Their banks had
come up with a high interest scheme that many charities
and councils had invested their reserves in. The scheme had
collapsed along with most other get rich schemes when the
financial crisis happened and the Icelandic banks couldn't
repay the money. It made the headlines at the time but very
little information had come out since. Doncaster had put
millions into it.

After the crash the government had agreed a massive bail
out through the International Monetary Fund (IMF) and the
European Union (EU) to repay the governments in Holland
and Britain who had both agreed to reimburse their residents
their investments in the scheme . . . . but the conditions attached
by the IMF and EU would decimate services and drive down

wages and living standards in Iceland. It would need each Icelandic citizen to pay 100 Euros a month for fifteen years, at 5.5% interest, to pay off a debt incurred by the bankers.

Workers organised massive demonstrations, riots broke out which forced the government to resign and new Left Wing government that condemned the previous governments economic policies was elected but in office they agreed the same bailout and conditions.

What happened next was extraordinary. The Icelanders refused to accept this, refused to be taxed to pay for the mistakes of a financial monopoly.

The Head of State, fearing the wrath of the people refused to ratify the law that would have made Iceland's citizens responsible for its bankers' debts, and accepted calls for a referendum.

The referendum was in March 2010 with 93% voting overwhelmingly to default on the debts instead of accepting austerity. The IMF froze the loan but the angry citizens had refused to accept the penalty so the government were forced to launch civil and judicial investigations into the responsibility for the economic crisis.

An international arrest warrant was issued for the ex-president of one of the banks as other terrified bankers fled the country 'obviously this is only a quick sketch of the reality' George said then continued with, but it didn't stop there. They wanted a new constitution so elected a committee of 25, none of who could belong to any political party to write a new constitution.

'Interesting possibilities here' he said.

John picked up on the point, he'd heard the same programme.

'Even the way the constitution's being written is revolutionary' he said. 'It's being done on line. Cyber-meetings are publicised and all residents can see the constitution being formed, comment make suggestions. Their remit is to 'free the country from the power of international finance and virtual money'

To misquote George 'We live in interesting times'

Many of the economies of Europe are struggling, workers facing massive attacks on their living standards to stabilise the Euro. Greece is on the verge of melt-down again. The IMF, the EU and the European Central Bank have bailed them out with €240bn in rescue funds in the past five years.

The country has seen its economy contract by close to 30%, its middle class decimated, its manufacturing base collapse, unemployment has reached record heights, with more than 26% out of work and its youth migrate, all as a result of tax increases and budget cuts demanded by lenders.

I can't see the Greeks accepting much more. It's no wonder the capitalist media are keeping silent about Iceland. The powers that be are terrified that it would soon spread throughout Europe. Workers in Britain are still stunned at the speed and ferocity of the onslaught of the jobs cull, destruction of services and the privatisation of the NHS through the back door that's been inflicted on them in the past few years.

Most of the economies of Europe are failing or risk failing, imperilling the Euro, with repercussions for the entire world, the powers that be don't want us to know what's happening in Iceland

All the main Parties pushing the same agenda and no-one challenging the need for austerity. The Labour Party failing to expose the lies of government.

An alternative of the Icelandic 'peoples revolt' could have been the spark that set other workers into action.

We should discuss this in more detail at a future meeting but we'll have to get some up to date information before then John finished

Grace was a bit stunned, she'd seen the sketchy reports on social media but hadn't followed it up to find out more except put Iceland in to the search engine But all she'd got was tourist adverts and it had slipped her mind.

They needed a new programme of discussions so she suggested discussing it the following week but said 'I'm not sure how much more there is to find on this so can I suggest we all do some research and we'll start the discussion with how a socialist society could be. I think writing the constitution on line with everyone being entitled to read, comment and contribute on it is a great idea for a democracy, let all decisions be made openly with maximum participation.

They always advertised their meetings on their media page and this had got more than usual comment. John had written,

> *Sick of austerity for the many and excessive profits for a few. It doesn't have to be like this. Come along to our meeting and hear about the Socialist alternative.*

Chapter 22

Grace arranged a speaker to come from Sheffield explaining about the discussion on Iceland and that all the members were trying to find out more about it but she asked if he would start the discussion on how things could be under socialism.

The followings week as she got to the meeting she was surprised to see faces she didn't know, it seems that the events in Iceland had inspired members and three had brought friends along. An outside speaker was of course an added attraction she thought.

Al was a good speaker and thought it a good idea to discuss how different it could be if the majority had a say in the running of the country. They were all so busy trying to get the message out there that they rarely talked further than the latest campaign.

He first explained the Socialist Party fights for a democratic society run for the needs of all not the profits of a few. WE oppose every cut and in our day to day campaigning for every possible improvement for the working class.

The organised working class has the potential power to stop the cuts and transform society. As capitalism dominates the globe the struggle

for genuine socialism must be international. We are part of the Committee for a Workers International, the CWI with organisations in 45 countries.

We would nationalise the top 150 companies and the banking system and bring transport, energy and communications back into the public domain. All to be run democratically by boards made up from the unions and service users. All representatives to be subject to recall and replacement if necessary.

A fully funded health service under democratic control run by a local board made up of hospital workers, service users and Trade Union reps.

A democratically planned low fare publically owned transport system a part of an overall plan against environmental pollution.

Medical research to be done to improve health not make profit, research shared nationally and internationally

A maximum 35 hour week

An end to nuclear power and major research into replacing fossil fuels with renewable energy

Free education and training available for all

For the right to asylum. Scrap all racist immigration laws.

A Massive house-building programme to provide home for the 2 million families in Britain without secure accommodation

An end to wars. Stop the production of weapons immediately. There are enough weapons available now to destroy the world many times over. Well we've only one world and our aim is to save and improve it

A democratic socialist plan of production based on the interests of the overwhelming majority and in a way that protects the environment. One where everyone has the opportunity to work and to take part in the decisions on what would be produced and how it would be distributed.

It sounds utopian but why?

I've no time to go in to it tonight and will gladly come back again to explain it further but at present in the UK and the rest of the world only about a third of the population do worthwhile work, millions unemployed or under-employed. Millions more working hard doing useless work and thousands of managers and owners who use all their energy finding ways to make more profit by driving the workforce harder or cutting back on safety.

Imagine if everybody worked how much lighter the work would be. Initially there is a lot of work needs to be done staffing the NHS and other services, house-building, fully staffed affordable public transport. But with everyone engaged we would soon achieve the basics of a decent life then if we found things running well and less workers needed we could cut the number of everyone hours, allow earlier retirement. Improve and expand leisure facilities.

Pensions and sick and disability benefits would reflect the cost of living so everyone benefits.

There is no blue-print for a socialist society because it would be truly democratic, I could only think of society being run by representatives from every level starting with streets, estates, villages, towns, regions up to government but Iceland are leading the way here. In the age of technology

All planning could be done in open forum on the internet. Anyone with the knowledge and interest could take part.

I'll use a quote from one of Claire's speeches at a public meeting a few years ago, I think she pinched it from John Lennon actually he said with a smile

'Imagine all the people sharing all the world'

Chapter 23

Another year was drawing to a close. Both Claire and Ellen were pregnant Claire was due to finish work soon Ellen had another three months to work but had reduced her hours. They were all coming tonight for possibly the last time because of the babies to let in the New Year

Things were moving now. They had organised on open meeting to discuss next year's election. It was a good turn-out. Most local activists had attended one group noticeable by their absent had decided to support the Labour Party to get rid of the Tories but everyone there expressed support for TUSC.

John led the discussion, explaining that Left formation, Socialist Alternative had had offered to pay the £500 deposit for all TUSC candidates standing in the general election and £500 towards the cost of leaflets for any candidates who had been a member of SA in the past which meant they could probably stand enough candidates in the local and general election to be entitled to a TV election broadcast. They wanted to stand 100 in the general election and 1000 for the council seats.

He asked for anyone interested in the general election or had suggestions of suitable candidates to speak up.

As previously arranged at their own branch meeting Grace volunteered as did a teacher who wasn't in SP. He would be an excellent candidate Grace thought. A former striking miner, long time activist, well respected in the town. A few other names were mentioned and all thought if one of the strikers of the privatised care workers would stand in the third seat in the district that they should go for it.

John went on to explain for the few who didn't know that TUSC didn't have individual membership as such, it was made up of different Trade Unionists and Socialist groups who had agreed to oppose all cuts and support a minimum socialist programme. It was run on federalist lines and within the programme each group or individual could plan their own leaflet.

In Doncaster the council elections would be interesting too as there had been some boundary changes and all the council seats were up for election so there were 54 local seats as well as the 3 parliamentary ones. John urged everyone present to think about standing in their local area. It would show they were a serious alternative to the cuts agenda of the mainstream Parties and an alternative to the racist Ukip.

It had been a good meeting and another was planned for early next year.

John and Grace were satisfied that TUSC was making headway, the Left in Doncaster were working well together. The people were desperate for a halt to the destruction of their essential services and the slashing of jobs and were disorientated that the Labour Party weren't offering any alternative.

Just before midnight John stood up to offer a toast to welcome in the New Year.

We live in interesting times, he started. We are involved in the formation of a new workers Party. We'll have a Party political broadcast which we can run on social media.

Raise a glass to a new dawn.